I STARTED GOING INTO CEMETERIES AND LOOKING AT TOMBSTONES . . .

I don't think I was overreacting. It wasn't that I expected Jacqui to be faithful or anything, or just only think of me, but the thought of my little boy trapped inside Jacqui and her talking about going prostituting was driving me crazy. I'd be driving along when I'd see a cemetery coming up ahead, and without really knowing it I'd turn in and spend an hour wandering among the tombstones. It was the only thing that made me feel peaceful.

"This is not for the squeamish."
—*The Chattanooga Times*

"Wonderfully strange, gruesome and funny."
—*Publishers Weekly*

"Jacqui is beauty and the beast rolled up in one. *Dearest* is for lovers of the macabre."
—*UPI*

DEAREST

PETER COUGHRAN

STEIN AND DAY/Publishers/New York

FIRST STEIN AND DAY PAPERBACK EDITION 1984
Dearest was originally published in hardcover
by Stein and Day/*Publishers* in 1983.
Copyright © 1983 by Peter Loughran
All rights reserved, Stein and Day, Incorporated
Designed by Louis Ditizio
Printed in the United States of America
STEIN AND DAY/*Publishers*
Scarborough House
Briarcliff Manor, N.Y. 10510
ISBN 0-8128-8082-X

DEAREST

Chapter

I should have known what Jacqui was like the second I set eyes on her. I should have been warned. One thing I've learned in life is you should always trust your first instincts about people. When you first meet them. That's when you can see right through people. Later on, when you get to know them better, you get confused and you make excuses for them. But when you meet someone for the very first time, what you notice then is what they almost always really are.

When she was alive, my mother always said, "Look at what a girl's wearing, son. A woman says everything about herself by what she puts on her back."

Jacqui was dressed right in the fashion. The fashion at that time was jeans with wide bottoms that came right down over your shoes. "Elephant's feet," they were called. The girls with short legs wore high heels underneath that couldn't be seen, so they looked as though they had very long, elegant legs. The tops of the trousers were supposed to be so tight they outlined the hairs on your backside, and girls with a bit of fat had a rear end like fifty-six pounds of jelly in a sock.

On top of that you were supposed to wear a little short pullover that didn't even come down to your belly button and left three inches of your stomach and back bare all around, and the sleeves only came halfway down to your wrists. That's what Jacqui was wearing the first time I met her.

Now you take someone who's like that, dressed right bang in the fashion, they're always a bolt or two short in the upper story. They're never what you'd call "good" women. The way they dress tells you a lot about their life-style. It's usually pretty boring. They read all the glossy mags (nothing else, just the glossy mags), and they look in the clothes shop windows everywhere you take them, and all they ever notice on the road is who's wearing what. It's a very dim way to be looking at life. You're not going to get much intelligent companionship from a woman like that. You're more likely to get a lot of trouble, in fact.

You see thousands of these little mod birds. They're always trailing around the streets trying to get themselves picked up. They're always bang up-to-date. One minute they're all trailing around in miniskirts, then it's maxis, then purple hot pants. They all look alike. They'd trail around in the nude with bananas on their head if that became the rage.

They're nearly always bad news. They hang around the firm where I work and take taxi rides just to try and make it with the drivers. You get one of them chucking herself at you about once a fortnight, on average, but I never take them up. I only normally like women who've got a bit of class, who are intelligent and different. One of the other lads at the firm, Chris, gets his leg over with them, and he often enough ends up smacking them around the mouth. He's always coming in saying how scruffy and slovenly they are around his flat. They've pulled some really charming things on him. One of them used to shove all her old female sanitary rubbish down the back of his bed rather than walk six steps to the lavatory and flush it away. Another used to shove everything in one of his saucepans, for the same reason.

It's not that I'm really terrifically fussy about girls. You get some blokes will only go out with tall blondes, or with petite brunettes, or slim girls, or girls with nice legs, or whatever. But I never go for one particular type. I find I like any shape or size so long as they have a few good points.

One, they've got to be clean. I can't stand scruffy women, or women who get dirty underneath and cover up the smell with perfume. My idea of scruffy is someone who doesn't have a shower or bath every day. I don't mind if the girl wears sloppy jeans or has her hair messed up, just so long as she's clean.

Then, I can't stand smokers. You get all these little birds running around chain-smoking all the time, that puts me right off. I never look twice at a bird with a cigarette. As soon as I see the little lighter and the little packet of fags in her hand, I just look the other way.

Besides those two things, I'm not usually fussy. If a girl's young and clean and doesn't smell like an ashtray, I'd usually find her attractive.

I meet a lot of women through my job. You often take women home in the cab, and then next week or so they're back looking for you. They fancy you. They don't try and pick you up the first time they meet you. Women aren't like that. That sort of thing only happens in the movies. A woman (a normal woman, not a slut or someone drunk), has to get to know a man before she's sure of herself. She keeps coming back and getting lifts with you. You've never seen her before, but all of a sudden you're giving her ten rides a week. Then she invites you in for a cup of coffee. They say there's more sins committed in the name of religion than anything else, but whoever said that, forgot coffee.

I'm not being bigheaded or anything, but usually I just keep it all friendly and platonic and keep my feet under the table and out of the bed sheets.

As often as not you don't fancy them. You just don't often meet a woman you really feel for, I mean one you

12

can enjoy it with and not be ashamed of yourself afterward.

There's some blokes can do it with anyone, but they're the sort who'd stand all day by a knothole in a fence.

For me, sex has got to be a tender kind of thing or it doesn't work. I've got to really like the woman before I even want to get started. If she's bent in some way, if she's itching for it, if she's all neurotic or anything, I just never even fancy the idea.

It's got nothing to do with looks. I had a girl friend once was really big and tubby, but she was absolutely beautiful. Liz, that was her name, was really full of fun and always laughing and telling jokes. If you read the women's magazines you'd think only girls built like paper clips are sexy, but that's a load of rubbish. Some birds with those model figures are about as rousing as a cold hot-water bottle with a leak. And some quite ordinary-looking girls are so beautiful they bring tears to your eyes.

Another thing wrong with Jacqui besides the mod clothes, she had bald eyes. I never before got serious with a girl with bald eyes. You know what I mean by "bald eyes?" It's when a girl messes about with her eyes so much she begins to look like a cat with the mange. She's always scraping away at her eyebrows with razor blades and tweezers, and she ends up with just a pencil line where the brows should be.

Then she has to get out the mascara bottle and paint everything black, all her eyelashes and everything. It was a popular fashion then, it was supposed to be glamorous. I always thought it just looked obscene, someone mutilating themselves like that. It was like those things they used to do in Africa years ago, putting plates in their lips and rings around their necks and bones in their noses.

Women messing around with their eyes don't only look bad, it's also a con trick. A really beautiful, intelligent woman has naturally fine eyebrows with a wide space in between them. She doesn't have to muck them about. But a lot of birds have got eyebrows like King Kong, so they chop at them worse than a guy with an ornamental hedge. They pluck them with tweezers and scrape them with razors until they've got this great big brutish growth off. Then they paint in a refined woman's face on top.

But there's still the ape woman underneath, the coarse, raunchy, unintelligent bird, and boy, do you find out if you get mixed up with her!

Later on, I saw some pictures of Jacqui when she was a young teenager, and she had eyebrows that practically went from ear to ear without a break. They gave her this deep heavy sullen look, which was her real character.

People think women paint their faces and muck about with themselves just to beautify themselves, but that's not the only reason. They do it to alter their whole character. They all know what a really gracious woman should look like, and they spend a fortune trying to look that way.

That's why so many blokes are disappointed in the woman they marry. They think they've married an angel, and they've got a chimpanzee.

A man should really analyze a woman. He should try

and see where she's changed her face, then put the real face back on and judge the woman's character from *that*. Not from the overhaul job.

As if mod clothes and chopped eyebrows weren't bad enough, Jacqui had these fancy fingernails, too.

You might not think that's too bad, a woman having fancy nails, but just think what it means to the bloke who's got to live with her. If a woman spends hours every day doing her nails, it means she's not doing anything else. She's not homemaking, knitting, sewing, cooking, baking pies, anything at all. She's just sitting scraping at her nails, or putting polish on them, or waving them around in the air to dry them, or mending chips in them, or taking the polish off again, or pushing back her cuticles.

You get the scene.

If you live with a fancy-nails woman, the rest of the house is barren. She won't do anything because she's too busy with her nails or she's scared of damaging them. So you live with unmade beds, uncleaned baths, unwashed dishes. You live out of tins and on packaged TV dinners and slimming foods you mix with skimmed milk. You live in a domestic desert.

All the love and all the tenderness and all the effort that a good woman puts into the home goes into your bird's bloody fingertips instead.

That's OK if all you want is a whore, but if you want a woman and a home, don't ever pick up with a bird who has fancy fingernails. A woman with fancy nails is a parasite.

When a man and a woman live together, it's usually a

working partnership. He does all the hard, heavy jobs, and she does the housework and makes things homey and beautiful.

I do a tremendous amount of work around the house, repairing the walls and roof, tending the garden, keeping the car running. When I have a girl friend, that's all *hers* to use. She can come and go in the house, sunbathe in the garden, borrow the car if she wants to. But if the woman's a fancy nail job, she's just like a leech. She takes everything and gives nothing back. She uses all your stuff, then leaves it messy and dirty.

When Jacqui was dead, I took all the red polish off her nails with remover and put on one of those very pale pink varnishes, and she looked much better.

I saw all those things, of course, when she turned up on our first date—and yet I didn't. I should have walked away then. I should just have gone off and left her. It would have saved her life at least, and I wouldn't have been half-murdered myself by what happened in between. I had half a mind to do it, and if I'd had my brains with me that day I'd have scooted.

The thing that made it hard to decide was she was good looking. A good-looking girl can pull the wool over a man's eyes anytime. Jacqui had classic looks. She had a very smooth face with big wide eyes and thick dark hair coming down onto her shoulders. She wasn't tarty like a lot of girls, all paint and powder with a little mean face back of all the camouflage. If you ignored the clothes and the nails and the eyebrows, she looked really nice. She had a look as though she was all the time blinking tears out of her eyes. I knew what that was about. A mate of hers, Tracey, had told me Jacqui was heartbroken over some guy who'd ditched her. I discovered why later on. He found out in time she was a tart. Afterward I was to think he was a very lucky man, he was able to get rid of her, but at the time I was fooled.

The problem is, no man can ever convince himself that a really beautiful girl could be a tart. A man always thinks a woman who looks like an angel must have the nature of an angel.

He wouldn't make the same mistake with another *man.* He knows that good-looking men can be slimy and two-faced. He often wonders how women are fooled by them, and then he's fooled himself by the same thing in a skirt.

I should have paid attention to all the things wrong with Jacqui. God knows, I had enough to go on. But then what bloke ever does notice everything he ought to? Where a good-looking girl's concerned, any man's a moron, and girls never get so good looking as at the age Jacqui was then, eighteen.

Girls only usually have one age when they're really sexy. That's around about seventeen or eighteen, till they're about twenty. Before that they're sort of hard and cold, and they act stupid, always being moody and going mad over pimply pop singers. And after they're twenty or so, they go off in another kind of way. They get sort of crafty and calculating. They stop thinking about love and romantic things, and they're always thinking about money. They're more like men than real women. Some of them even grow moustaches.

But you take a girl in the middle of those two times, she can be really lovely. Even very ordinary-looking girls can be absolute knockouts for just that year or two. It's Nature that does it. She makes the girl flower, just like a bush of roses. When she's growing up she's just a skinny little stem, and when she's over the top she goes all hard and thorny. But in between, she can be like velvet. She's a really lovely thing. She gives off a sort of perfume from her skin that just makes you want to kiss her all over. She goes a lovely shape, coming out in all the right places and going in all the places she should. She fills a blouse so beautifully you feel you could spend a million pounds on her.

When she gets sexy, she sort of fills up with blood. Her lips go a lovely purple color and red-hot, and her eyes go very deep and yearning.

What man can turn down a deal like that, no matter what his brain says?

The only safe thing is to judge a woman more by what you find underneath than on top. It's a funny thing about girls, they're either much better underneath than on the surface, or much worse. You get some real surprises. The last girl I had before Jacqui was like that. That was Ilse. She was a German au pair. On the outside she looked really very ordinary. She looked the sort of girl who'd work in a library or an insurance office: glasses, old-fashioned clothes, all that. But underneath she was incredibly beautiful. She had a figure like one of those slim little Victorian statues you see in the gardens of big old houses, where they're sitting by fountains and things, with a perfect little bust and beautiful smooth legs. I used to love just to look at her in the firelight. When she'd come around I'd get her to wear her bikini in the house, just so I could see how nice she was all the time.

Jacqui was the other way around. Oh, she looked quite glamorous enough dressed up, high bust, slim waist, long legs and all that, but it was really all just a makeup job.

She was very hairy, for a start. She had to shave all over her legs every other day, from the top to the bottom, because of this heavy growth of hair she'd had from a young teenager. Half the time, when you were stroking her legs, she had either this too-smooth feel that wasn't natural, or she had a really sharp stubble. Her upper lip was the same. She was always plucking at it and shaving it, but sometimes when you kissed her, it was like tiny little needles.

Her back had a sort of pattern on it, too, there were so many hairs on it they made sworls, like flocked wallpaper.

Then she had these peculiar ankles. She didn't really have an ankle at all, as a matter of fact. Her calf just carried on thick down to her foot, like an animal's fetlock, and on the end she had these big lumpy feet, all bent from being shoved into shoes that didn't fit her.

The thing is, if you'd judged Jacqui from the outside

you'd have thought she was a nice, fresh girl, much prettier than the average, in fact. But if you could have seen what was underneath right away, if you could have had all her clothes and her camouflage off the first second you met her, you'd have seen she could have been a bit bestial, and you'd have believed she had the makings of a prostitute.

I spent a lot of time in the next seven months thinking about prostitutes (I couldn't help myself, really, the way Jacqui kept rubbing my nose in it), and I sort of worked out what I thought was a good reason why a woman might turn into one.

It seemed to me the problem was that all women are basically inclined that way; it's their instinct to give their sexuality for profit, for some kind of gain.

It's normal enough. A woman's got to have material things to bring up the children, she's got to have shelter for them, food, clothes. And all that takes money. So no sane woman will give herself sexually unless she's sure of getting some sort of material return. Any woman who breaks that rule ends up in a right mess. She marries a guy who can't provide and spends the rest of her life living in two rooms in a slum, scratching for pennies and dressing the kids out of jumble sales.

But it's still a form of prostitution isn't it? It's still trading sex for money.

You see it clearer if you think of the opposite, a bloke bedding with a girl and her giving *him* money. It's against all a man's instincts. He feels disgusted with himself. He's a gigolo, a pimp, the lowest form of animal life. But what's sick for a man is normal for a woman. It just goes to show you the difference between the two.

So it's a normal thing for a woman to be a bit inclined that way. The problem with Jacqui was, she was more like that than she should have been. She went over the top. There was something wrong with her instincts, like they were subnormal or mongoloid or something. Maybe she had something wrong in her brain. Maybe all women who screw around have something wrong with their brain cells.

Normal women sell themselves to just one man. They have a sort of mechanism that stops them screwing with just anyone. They fall in love, or feel a sense of responsibility, and that stops them getting involved with anyone else. Their sexuality switches itself off. You get that everywhere you go. You see a really nice girl you'd like to get to know better, and then one of your mates tells you she's not available, she's in love with someone else. It's not that she's *trying* to be faithful to her husband or whoever it is, it's just that she really is switched off towards other men. She doesn't even notice them, and you could chat her up till you were blue in the face and it wouldn't make any difference. It's just a natural mechanism.

Life would be bedlam without it, if everyone kept getting sexy all over the place. But some people don't have it, and that's what makes a rapist or a flasher in the park. Or a pro like Jacqui. That's what I think, anyway.

I just wish I'd realized all that at the time, when I first met Jacqui. But I didn't. I only saw the outside, and I ended up taking her out for the day. I took her out to a restaurant in the country, then back to my place in the evening.

Some blokes always invite a new bird to a party when they first meet her. Maybe they're nervous or something and they can't face the girl on their own, they've got to have a crowd. Or maybe they're just trying to impress: The "I've got a million pals" act.

But I've never bothered with parties. I can always find a woman at work, I don't need to have get-togethers. I've only once given a party in my life, and was I sorry!

Once you've found a woman you like, what's the point of having fifty other people with you when you meet her? If you've got a serious date with a woman, it should always be a twosome.

And always take her wining and dining. It's about the only thing most women are really interested in. That, and going looking at the fashions in the shops. They'll go for a walk in the country with you if they really like you. They'll even go to an art gallery if they're determined to impress. But their little hearts aren't in it. They're much happier just sitting in a restaurant eating and drinking, provided they're not worrying about their diets and their figures.

If you want a woman to like you, feed her. That's just nature too. You see it all the time with the birds in the garden. When the female gets the hots for the male she pretends she's a baby, and he stuffs food down her beak. It's worms and caterpillars with him, and it's steaks and salads with you, but it gets the same result.

It's a good idea, too, to combine the meal with a trip

out. That way the girl gets a nice drive and a look at the country. That usually bowls them over. Most women are very stuck-in-one-place. If they live in town, they haven't been out in the country for years. It never seems to occur to them. They seem quite happy going back and forth to the shops and never getting a breath of fresh air or resting their eyes with a decent view. It really impresses them, usually, when they see fields and woods and country lanes. It's very relaxing. It does you a lot of good.

I took Jacqui to this country restaurant in Kent, down by Maidstone. I knew it from taking a party down there in the summer. You can have a nice lunch, right on the riverbank. The dining room's all glass, and you can sit there eating and watch the boats sailing past. Just outside the pub there's a weir that's all the time making this rushing sound like a waterfall. It's very soothing when you spend a lot of time driving in town. Then, when you've had your lunch, you cross the river, and there's an old castle on the other side. It's run by monks, and they show you all over it for a few bob. The whole place is furnished just as it must have been hundreds of years ago. It's really a nice place to visit, if ever you want a good day out.

I took her out by car, of course. You should never take a girl out by bus or train. Nothing kills a good relationship quicker than sitting in some dreary, freezing station waiting for some smelly train full of fag ends to roll up an hour-and-a-half late because it's Sunday and the workmen are fixing the tracks. If you take a girl out, take her in your own car, or don't bother.
And make sure your car's decent looking and clean.

There's few things a woman hates more than being picked up in a tatty old wagon with all the paint chipped and six months' dirt on the carpets.

A woman likes a good car. A car to a woman isn't just a machine to get around in. I don't think she even thinks of it as a machine at all. I mean, women hate machines but love cars. A car to a woman is exactly the same thing as a hat or a dress or a pair of shoes, she'll love it if it's smart and nice, but she'll hate it if it's shabby.

The car I had then was a late-model Cortina GT in flame red with a gold coach line. It was quite a nice machine. I had it on wide wheels and tires, and it handles really decently. I kept it really clean, too. I washed and polished and hoovered it at least once a week. If you do that regularly a car gets a really beautiful look to it, all glossy and clean, like you could measure the shine with a ruler.

Jacqui was a pain the whole day. She was OK while we were in the car with the heater on, or sitting in the restaurant, but every time we went out in the air she was squealing about it being cold. I was really enjoying myself. Cold frosty air in the country smells fantastic; it makes you want to run and shout like a little kid. But Jacqui, with her stupid clothes on, was all the time miserable and wanting to get back in the car. The river and the castle looked marvelous, but she had about as much appreciation for them as a cow would have for your living room carpet.

When I saw Jacqui carrying on like that it should have been another warning. She *knew* she was going out to the

24

country for the day, she only had to look out of her bedroom window to see it was frosty. Yet she turned up with next to nothing on to keep her warm. On top of her pelvis-crusher jeans and half a pullover, she only had a little curly sheepskin jacket that was so small she couldn't fasten it over her chest. No scarf, no gloves, no hat, no nothing. She wasn't wearing knickers. She didn't want to look fat. And she had no socks on her feet, her shoes were so tight she couldn't get any on.

And that's another sign a woman isn't all there, when she wears shoes too small for her. You get these women who go in shoe shops and tell the assistant they're size six, when all the time they're an eight. Then they spend two hours trying to shove their great big feet into shoes that wouldn't fit if they had all their toes amputated. A woman who carries on like that isn't all there. She's out of touch with reality, living in a dream world. Kidding yourself to that extent is halfway to being off your rocker.

I thought I'd seen enough. I thought, "This one isn't going anywhere."

I was all set to drop her off back at the end of her road and not bother seeing her again. I had it all planned in my mind when I stopped at a service station to fill up for the return journey, and before I realized it, Jacqui had run across to the cash desk and paid the bill.

That threw me somehow, it put me right off my stride. You must make a judgment on a girl, and then she goes and does a nice thing like paying for your petrol. How many women do you take out who ever offer to pay for your petrol? And without being asked?

How many women ever offer to pay for *any*thing?

Most women think they're doing you a big favor, going out with you at all. If they don't turn up more than half-an-hour late, they reckon they've been really good. A lot of girls only go out with blokes at all because it costs them nothing.

"Ah well," they think, "it's better than sitting home watching the telly, and I'll get a free meal and a trip out."

They think maybe they'll let you have a little fumble at the end of the day, just to pay you for everything. But you never see their handbags open. Except to get their mirrors out and look at their faces now and then.

So what Jacqui did really threw me. I tried to give her the money back, I tried to push it in her hand. But she didn't want to take it, she even put her hands behind her back.

"No," she said, "you've given me a lovely day." And she had all these tears brimming up in her eyes again.

What could I do after that except take her home. When a nice-looking girl does a generous thing like paying for your petrol, and she's got tears in her eyes, you can't just ditch her. I forgot the bald eyes, the fancy nails, the mod clothes, and everything they meant, and I took Jacqui back to my place.

Months afterward, I used to get very spooky feelings about it. You know, like in a murder movie, and the girl's going into the house, and you know she's going to get killed, and the music goes all eerie. I'd see a replay of Jacqui coming into my house, with a piano following her footsteps, and shots of shadows moving in dark corners, and things like that.

I've wished a million times it had never happened. You could wish your life away on things like that. Things you wished you hadn't done, people you'd never bumped into. I kept thinking of the thousand-and-one other things I could have done instead of taking her home.

It reminds me of this story we read at school called "Paths of Destiny." It's about this bloke who has a chance of three different roads in life, and each one he takes only leads to the same end, he gets shot with the same pistol.

That was a really brilliant story. Maybe life's like that. Maybe everyone has a destiny, sort of some place he has to arrive at, and no matter what he does, he ends up there.

We had a lad at the taxi firm once who used to be a lorry driver, and one day when he was driving his truck he killed a woman pushing a pram and her little girl who was walking alongside her. He killed all three of them, the baby in the pram as well. He scraped them against this massive great wall that ran along the pavement.

It nearly drove him mental. All he could talk about was, "Why didn't I take another road, why didn't I take another turning?" He kept telling us he'd meant to turn off way back, or he thought he'd buy a paper, but didn't. In the five minutes leading up to the accident, there were about ten thousand permutations of things he could have done, and only one of them ended up in the accident.

And of course, there were another ten thousand permutations for the woman and her kids. If only she'd left the house thirty seconds earlier or later. If only the little girl had wanted a tinkle-stop somewhere. If only the baby had thrown its rattle out of the pram, and the mother had had to stop and pick it up. Or maybe that was *why* they were there at that exact moment, maybe all those things had happened.

It all drove him nearly crazy.

It wasn't even *his* fault. Some tear-ass shot out of an intersection and smashed right into his front wheels and sent the lorry onto the pavement. The driver was one of those hot-shot little middle-management salesman types who are always such a pain on the roads. They always want to be overtaking, weaving in and out. They cause about ninety-nine percent of all the accidents you ever see.

But even that silly little git might have been part of his destiny. I don't know. It's all very complicated.

Of course, that's the big moment, when you take a girl back to your place and she agrees to go. It means you've come to an understanding about one another. If you say to a girl, "Shall we go around to my place?" you've basically said to her, "I'd like to get you somewhere private where we can have a chance of getting sexy."

And if she says "Yes," she's saying, "I think you're a likable sort of bloke and I'm willing to give it a go, if you are."

In the evening, you should always take a woman home, never out. It's okay to take a woman to a restaurant for lunch, but you should never make the mistake of taking her out to eat in the evening.

When you have an evening meal with a woman, always do it at home.

If you take her out, there's always too much hassle. The weather might be wet or cold, the thing she wants is off the menu, the place is crowded, and you have to wait an hour to get served. Then, when you've finished the wining and dining, you've got to trail her home to a cold house with "Screwsville" written all over you.

It's much better if you take the girl back to your place right at the beginning. Everything's very homey and nice. And when the end of the evening comes, you're in this lovely warm house by the fire.

And if you live in a very nice house, that helps your case no end, too. You get blokes practice all kinds of stunts to attract birds. They do the cultured gentleman bit, or they dress flashy and carry a big roll of fivers. Or they have the sports car, with the big red phallic-symbol bonnet, or they practice a hot line in chatting up.

Every bloke you ever meet practices some kind of stunt he thinks is going to attract the birds.

My mother said, "You'll have this big house when I'm gone, and that will bring the girls running."

A really nice house is the best bird-getter of all. Especially if you live there on your own. Nothing gets you places faster than that. The thing is, women have this nesting instinct, they can't wait to get hold of some place and take it over. They want somewhere to do their breeding in. They come into a great big house like mine and their little minds go "Wow!" They look at the hall

29

and the big staircase with all the carved rails, and they think how marvelous it would be to get their hands on all this. Then they realize at the back of their minds that it *could* all be theirs. All they've got to do is make you fall in love with them, and you'll *give* it to them.

That's one of a woman's chief aims in life, to get a bloke to give her a house. There's hardly a woman in the world would thank you for saying this, but that's how most of them get their houses. They don't buy them or build them or anything, they just get some guy to give them one. They paint themselves up to look really attractive and sexy, the guy falls for them, and "bingo!" they've got the house.

That's why a woman is usually so keen to get the guy to the altar, and not just live with him. It's not morals. It's just that, without the marriage certificate, she's got no claim on the dwelling. If they're not married and the guy cools off, he can get rid of her and she's got no rights at all to the bricks and mortar.

So a good house works wonders for you with a woman, without your even trying.

I'm lucky like that, I live in a sort of Victorian mansion like something out of a Sherlock Holmes movie. My mother inherited it from Mr. Williamson, the old boy she used to work for, as his housekeeper. My dad left home when I was about two, and I never had any brothers and sisters, so since my mother died I've lived in it on my own. It's sort of peaceful that way. The house is very big, with a huge staircase in the hall and lots of rooms and cellars.

There's a circular drive in front with masses of shrubbery and a back garden you could get lost in.

Mostly I keep it all to myself. I did try sharing it once or twice, but it was hopeless. I had this couple in who used to leave the kitchen looking like a pigsty, and when I got rid of them, there was another bloke who got drunk all the time and never wanted to pay any rent. After that I decided to live on my own. That way I could keep the house decent and live peacefully, without all sorts of morons messing it up and bringing their dirty habits into it.

I'm really very fond of the house. It's a sort of hobby with me. When I've done a stint in the taxi I like nothing better than to get home and do a quiet bit of work on the property. There's something really beautiful about having a big house all around you, and just the trees swishing in the breeze, with no traffic or trannies or people babbling everywhere.

I never got married.

I suppose the reason is, I've never felt sexy enough to be married. Oh, I like a girl in bed as much as the next man, but that's not really what I mean by being sexy. You take the average guy, you'll see what I'm getting at.

The average guy, from the time he's a teenager, he's thinking of hardly anything else but sex. He's dressing up all the time and combing his hair and worrying about his appearance. He spends all his time at discos and pubs trying to attract birds.

He's *got* to have a wife. If he can't get a nice one, he'll marry any old thing. She could be built like the back end of a London Transport bus garage and have a temper like a rhinoceros with piles, but he'll lead her to the altar like she's Cleopatra or the Queen of Sheba.

Then, when he's got the wife, he goes mad on breeding. That's the chief thing in his life. He'll do any old job he hates, just so he can get the money to keep his woman and kids, pay for the house, and all the rest of it. He's desperate for sons and daughters, and it absolutely breaks his heart if he can't have them. When he's got kids, he's obsessed with them. He talks about how they've got a new tooth and how they've learned to use the potty, and all kinds of rubbish. His mind's completely taken up with sex and breeding. If he doesn't get a woman by the time he's thirty, he turns into an alcoholic and sits around paralytic all day in bars and goes home at night to a tiny flat that looks like a storeroom for dandruff.

I'm not like that. I can live on my own quite happily. I never was mad keen on the idea of breeding. I always found it a right little off-putter, in fact. You know what they say: "A wife's a woman who helps a man bear the troubles he wouldn't have if he hadn't married her." Well, that could be my motto.

Marriage with kids always struck me as degrading, in fact. You pick a lot of families up in the cab, and it can be very depressing. There's the poor little pathetic father, forty-five years old and doesn't look a day over sixty. He looks as though he's spent the last twenty years in a concentration camp. Which is what marriage is, when you think about it. You can't get out, you're worked half to death, the food's lousy, and you don't get paid a penny for it.

And everywhere a married man goes he's got this bunch of kids trailing around after him. Sometimes they're young, which isn't so bad. Little kids can be very cute and sweet. But if they're grown teenagers, you can usually bet they're a complete pain in the ass, you can bet they really despise their father. He's only spent half his life looking after them, spending all his money on them, so they're sort of honor-bound to hate his guts. They either think he's a pathetic little runt who couldn't be trusted to blow his own nose, or they hate him because he's always the big shot and trying to boss them around. There's hardly ever a civil word between teenagers and their parents, except when the kids are on the scrounge for money, then they can be sweet enough. They poison the atmosphere in the car. Give me a couple of unmarried lads or girls any day. They laugh and joke and they have fun, which is something families hardly ever do.

So marriage is something I've never been very keen on. I just go from girl friend to girl friend. I never really ever plan sex, I just sort of drift into it. I can be without a girl friend for months, then I'll get a nice one in the taxi, we'll click, and we'll go out together for as long as the thing's got life in it.

That seems to be about three months, mostly. At the end of three months you usually just seem to drift apart again. I never could think of any particular reason why. You just start seeing less and less of one another, till one day you're not seeing each other at all anymore.

When things reach that stage, I always buy the girl a really nice present, something worth a bit of money and care, to show I appreciate us having been friends. I bought Ilse a beautiful little figurine of a nude girl by a pool, to remind her of how beautiful I always thought she was. It's my way of saying "thank-you" to them for a nice time.

Some people might say that's a selfish way to live, but what about blokes who marry, then? They're only pleasing themselves. Most of them get married to one woman because one woman's all they can ever attract. And besides, they're nobodies. They're only little guys and they're not very brainy. No one's scared of them, and no one takes any lip from them. But they want to be boss somewhere, to be lord of the manor. So they get married, have kids, and turn into little Hitlers inside their own four walls. I could never be like that. I treat all the women I'm fond of with decency and appreciation.

As soon as I got in the house with Jacqui, I started getting a meal ready. That's good for two things. One, if a woman's impressed with *one* good meal in a day, she'll be ten times as impressed with two.

When you come into the house, you should always find something to do to break the ice. Get away from the girl and let her get her bearings. If you hang around her chatting and all that, you can mess things up.

I always get the girl to light the fire in the big sitting room. Everything's there, kindling, logs, matches. It gives her something to do. It makes her feel she belongs.

You tell her where the bathroom is as well, so she can use it while your back's turned. Most women don't like you to see them using the lavatory.

Then you go into the kitchen and make a noise, so she knows where you are, then she can do all her private things in peace.

You should always let her know where you are. You'd be surprised how many women think batchelors have peepholes drilled in the walls, and hidden cameras. There must be guys do that sort of thing. Some people are so bent it's almost unbelievable.

One thing you should never do is make it look the typical seduction scene. You know, the bottle of wine, the mood music, all that kind of stuff. A man and a woman go out together so they can have sex together, but it shouldn't be too obvious. The best thing of all is when you like each other so much you just sort of fall into each other's arms with your hearts going twenty to the dozen. But that doesn't happen very often. Usually you've got to warm to each other and trust each other.

But you should never be obvious. I went out with a girl once who was obvious, and it was terrible. I never saw her again, it was so embarrassing. I reckon she was just a scalp collector. She probably kept a diary on all the blokes she'd screwed with. She arranged for me to go around to her place and she served me up a great big steak dinner. She probably reckoned I was going to need the strength. There was a bottle of wine too. They say wine's good for giving a woman sex appeal, if you put it inside the man. Then when we'd finished eating, she plonked herself down on the couch by the fire and pulled her skirt halfway up her thighs to let the air at her legs.

I took her for a drive. We went miles across country in all this deep snow. Anything rather than bed a woman who made it so obvious. If she'd been subtle I could have fancied her. She was very cute and pretty, and only about twenty.

I cooked the meal for Jacqui myself. I always keep these sorts of dinners very simple but serve up really nice food. My mother was a brilliant cook, and she showed me how to do just about everything.

The golden rule to remember is to make it all nonfattening. Every girl you ever meet has an absolute bee in her bonnet about calories. If you serve up a meal she thinks is going to put weight on her, she won't touch it. Or if she does eat it she'll feel bad about it, and that won't do either of you any good.

The golden rule is, keep away from heavy food and serve only good stuff. I've got a big chest freezer in the kitchen and I always keep a lot of things there, chops, chickens, steaks, roasts, burgers, peas, sprouts, things like that. I roasted a chicken for Jacqui, but first I took off all the fat, and before I served it up I skinned it. With that I did a salad of green peppers, onions and mushrooms, with a dressing of wine vinegar and sunflower oil. There was fresh fruit to follow, and with the meal I gave her a glass of Mâcon Rouge. (I always keep a few bottles of good wine in the house.)

When you serve the wine you should always say to the

girl, "Just one glass, hey? It's very strong and it might go to your head." (I discovered later on Jacqui had a head like a cast-iron kitchen range for drink. She could get through a whole bottle of wine as though it was cherryade. When she was pregnant I had a hell of a job stopping her poisoning the kid.)

Nothing looks worse than a guy plying a girl with drink. And anyway, it's dead wrong to get a girl drunk for sex. Like I said, it should be a tender sort of thing.

You should always be very careful to taste all the food in front of the girl and sample the wine, to show her it's not drugged. You don't tell her that's why you're doing it, of course, but you can bet at the back of her mind she's thinking it might be. You hear all kinds of stories about these creeps who try to drug girls when they take them out.

The usual way is to fill them full of drink. You know, "After ten double brandies, she's anyone's." But you get guys push reefers onto them, give them pills to pop. And there's always the odd nutter uses sleeping pills or chloroform.

When we'd finished eating, I got a couple of brandies in balloon glasses, and we sat by the living room fire to see if something would happen. Men and women meet each other for sex. All the rest is only padding, the trips, the meals, the walks, the theaters. The real business of the day starts when you arrive some place, yours or hers, where you can be on your own and get intimate.

Not that I was expecting anything with Jacqui. I'd much sooner have waited awhile. If a woman's too quick with it you only start thinking she must be a pushover. It doesn't do *her* any good, and it doesn't do *you* any good. A hundred to one if that happens the first or second time the bloke will only throw it up in the girl's face later on. He'll always think, "If she let *me* have it so easy, she'll be the same with other blokes."

And, of course, the girl will think the same way.

Ilse and me waited the best part of two months, and I really respected her for it. She wanted to be sure she was doing the right thing.

But with Jacqui it all happened very quickly. We were sitting by the fire together playing chess (it's funny, but Jacqui enjoyed playing chess), when suddenly this great big tear rolled down her face and splashed on the board. I guessed she was thinking about her broken love affair. I had an idea what she was feeling.

I'd felt the same way about Ilse. She'd gone back to Germany to marry her childhood sweetheart. It was one of those things arranged by both families since they were just toddlers. Ilse didn't want to do it, but she felt she owed it to her mother and father. I'd been missing Ilse a lot since she'd gone, so I had an idea what was going on in Jacqui's head.

"Pretty bad is it, girl?" I said, and the next thing I knew she was hanging on to me and sobbing all over me. She didn't say anything, she just kept pouring out the tears so I was all soaked through my shirt. I quietened her down after a while and got her to tell me all about it, about this Jim feller she'd had an affair with. It seems she'd met him at a party and ended up in bed with him the first night. He was about fifty-five and she was eighteen. It was a really weird story. He was living with someone else at the time (a German woman, funnily enough), near his own age, but he'd bring Jacqui around all the time, kissing her and cuddling her in public and telling everyone she was going to be his wife. They were party set people, and Jim made big money in advertising. Jacqui was really wowed by it all.

She said it was like a beautiful glamorous dream, all these people coming and going, drinking cocktails, and partying till the early hours every morning. The German woman apparently didn't try and stop it, she was just very nice to Jacqui.

Of course, it all crashed. One day he just wouldn't see her anymore, and she was brokenhearted. It seems he was impotent. At the time it sounded very much like he'd tried it with a young girl to ginger himself up and it hadn't worked, so he'd called it off. The German woman was probably helping him, letting him use young girls to try and get him out of his problem.

Later on though, when Jacqui had told me about the other blokes she was screwing with at the same time, I saw things a bit differently. It could be that Jim fancied the "pure young girl" image, and when he found out Jacqui was banging half the town, he lost interest.

I should have gone off her myself at that point. It should have been obvious she was a bit nuts. The way she told me the story about Jim, it was all magic and glamorous. She didn't seem to realize how sordid it was. She didn't seem to realize he was just an old geezer pushing sixty and not much else. You can imagine the poor old bugger when he stripped, worried to death he wasn't going to manage it and make a pill of himself in front of this young bird.

And I could see another danger looming up in front of me too. Unless I was very much mistaken, me and this girl were going to be having it off inside about twenty minutes. And once you do that you really get in deep water. They say a man with a woman should be like a bear with a bee's nest, he should grab the honey and get away before he's stung. A wise man gets what he came for and then gets out.

But I never could be like that. I only ever knew one girl I could have sex with and not miss her till the next time I saw her. That was a girl called Angela. She was a lovely girl, very sweet natured and all that, but I just never missed her when she was gone. We had some really nice times together, but once I'd driven her home I never worried about her till the next time I saw her. Usually, if I like a girl enough to go to bed with her, then the next day I find myself phoning her to see how she's getting on.

That's natural enough, really. If you like a girl well enough to do something really important and intimate with her like having sex, then you're bound to be concerned about her in other ways. If you're not, then maybe it's a sign you're cheapening the whole sex thing. Or you're the sort of person who never worries about anyone but himself, who just uses other people for his pleasure.

But what can you do? You've got a good-looking girl snuggled up to you, you're in a big house all alone together in front of the fire, and she's all warm and soft from crying. There's usually only one thing you *do* do at a time like that, and I did it. You *should* be sensible about it. You *should* ask yourself if you're not going to land yourself in hot water, but you don't, do you? If brains were stronger than balls, no one would ever get married. The human race would have died out before the Stone Age.

I got another warning there, too, as if I hadn't already had enough of them. That was the way Jacqui acted when we finally *did* get started.

If you can tell a lot about a girl from the way she dresses and makes up, then you can tell even more by how she behaves the first time you have sex with her. A girl having sex is like a drunk with a bottle, the whole character comes out, and you can make up your mind then what's the best thing to do for the future.

Take the expert bra-flicker. I never go any further with them. You take a girl home and she's all innocent and fluttering eyelashes. Then, when clothes-off time comes and you're fumbling with her straps, she just reaches behind her and "flick," the way's open. You look at her and she's got a face on her like a bus driver, she's done this route so many times she hardly needs to be awake to follow it.

That's a right off-putter. Sex between a man and a woman should be a lovely sort of a high, not something you do so often you get bored stiff with it. With a bra-flicker you feel as though you should be buying a timetable.

I can't stand that type. I brought a woman like that home to the house once, and I still wince when I think of it. She fooled me. She didn't look like a bra-strap flicker. She looked very classy, in fact. She was dressed really beautifully, and she talked like a private school.

But when I got her on the bed and started fumbling for the catches, she went through like a signalman shifting points. She really knew all the levers to pull. She didn't only flick the bra off, she flicked off everything else as well.

I went all cold. I thought, "Gee whiz, there's been more traffic through here than through the Dartford Tunnel."

What I did was pretend to fall asleep. I certainly wasn't going to touch her. I made like I'd gone asleep—worn out with working late—and after about half an hour she put everything back on again. She must have had more gooseflesh than a freezer full of chickens. She never came to see me again. I was glad. I really don't like her type at all.

Then there's the "only through the cloth" variety. I only ever met one of them, but if you meet one, there must be others around. You could do what you liked with her, but you weren't allowed to go past the cloth. She had a fiancé—in the Royal Marines I think it was—and that was her idea of being faithful to him!

I didn't like it. I found it really unnatural. After one try I'd had enough and gave it up. It was a bit like trying to comb your hair with your hat on.

Then there's the orgasm bird. She's been reading all

these magazine articles about how *every* woman should have an orgasm and how it's her *right,* and if she can't get it with one bloke she should try another.

You meet a lot of them. All she can think of when she's with you is bringing herself off. She's thrashing around in the bed and moaning and wriggling around underneath you, trying to find her moment. It's like trying to have it off with a rubber dinghy.

She couldn't give a damn about *you* or your feelings. You can try really hard to give her a good time, but if she doesn't have the sort of orgasm they call the fire engines to she's as sarcastic as hell all evening. Women's rights she's red-hot on, men's rights she's never even heard of.

Another one is the "history teacher." She thinks the best way she can help you along is to tell you in detail about all the other blokes she's done the same thing with, and how good they were. I think she marks everyone out of ten. Size, reach, stamina, and all that. I get nought out of ten every time, for not even attempting the exam and sloping out the bedroom door.

Girls who are just nice and loving in bed, without more hangups than a hedgehog's got fleas, are few and far between. That's why there's so many blokes packing the pubs. If they had a good woman, they'd be at home.

Jacqui of course, she was different to anyone I'd ever met before. She wasn't a bra-flicker or an orgasm bird or a history teacher. She just *died* on me. One minute I had a live woman talking to me, and the next I had a corpse. I carried on, thinking she'd wake up, but she just *lay* there.

Even her hands just lay open on the carpet, as though she was dead. I was looking at her face really closely in the firelight, and there was absolutely nothing in her eyes at all. Most girls make some kind of response, even if only to tell you to stop it, but Jacqui was just like a zombie.

It was a real off-putter. There we were, doing what must be the most intimate thing two people can possibly ever do together, and she was showing about as much life as a British Rail salad. She was getting less pleasure out of sex than she would out of brushing her teeth.

I realized, afterward, that's what a prostitute must be like, she must be someone who gets nothing out of sex. If you get nothing out of a thing, you don't much mind who you share it with. If you had a ratty old lawnmower, you wouldn't much mind who you lent it to. But if you had a really beautiful job, you'd only want to lend it to someone you really liked.

I think sex is like that. Sex to me is a beautiful thing, so I couldn't do it with a slut, or for money, or even with someone I wasn't really very fond of. But I suppose there are people who don't think sex is a very good thing, they don't respect and don't value it, so they can do it with anyone.

Months later, when Jacqui went on the game and I was really in despair about it, she told me having sex wasn't important to her, it was just a bodily function, like eating. "You wouldn't be fussy who you sat down to table with," she said, "so why be fussy who you go to bed with?" I think it's that attitude makes a prostitute. They use sex

44

tattily, because to them sex is something without any value.

After a minute or two I came out of her and just lay alongside her.

"I'm sorry," I said, "but I can't do it with a zombie. I like you a lot, you're a lovely girl, but I need a bit of encouragement."

I said it really gently, I mean, she was being nice to me and I didn't want to hurt her feelings. But then she *really* started crying. She nearly choked herself. I had to spend hours nursing her while she sobbed all over me, and this time it was my *skin* got all wet because I didn't have any clothes on.

I should really have taken that as another warning. She'd got herself screwed up before she'd met me, and she was going to get herself screwed up again.

I made another rule for myself after that, to stick in my little book: "Never feel sorry for a bird who's only feeling sorry for herself."

That's all Jacqui was doing, really. It wasn't as if she was upset about someone else's problems, about people starving in Africa or the threat of World War Three, she was just carrying on because her party set of boozers had chucked her.

People like that are just imposing on your sympathy. I had a fare I picked up just before I met Jacqui, and he pulled that stunt on me. He was all bandages and plasters. He had a bandage around his head, plasters all over his face, and his arm in a sling. I took him three miles to his house. It was a no-profit job really, the traffic was thick, and I wouldn't have made a penny even if he *had* paid his fare.

But when we got to where he lived, he tried to rip me off. He sat in the car for five minutes, groaning and groping in his pockets, pulling out 10 pence here and 10 pence there. It was a pure bloody con trick. He was waiting for me to get embarrassed and say, "That's all right, mate, don't bother." I wouldn't mind betting he had a wad of notes in his inside pocket. He was cashing in on the bandages, getting everything he could for nothing. He told me he'd been in a car accident. I reckon it was more likely he'd been thumped for some mean little stunt he'd tried to pull on someone.

I should have felt the same way about Jacqui; I should have saved my sympathy for people who deserved it.

But it had exactly the opposite effect. What it did was make me fall in love with her.

You take a thing like that, a big grown girl of eighteen crying helplessly all over you, there's no quicker way to lose your heart. You can fall in love quicker with a woman who's brokenhearted than with any other kind. The thing is, you get the feeling she's at the bottom, she needs you desperately, she's not going to survive without you.

I felt about Jacqui like I'd feel about a little child drowning. Sometimes, when you're down at the coast, you stand on the pier watching all the people mill about, and you wonder what you'd do if one of the little kids got pushed in the water. You'd go in after him, wouldn't you?

46

It wouldn't matter if the water was thirty feet down and there was a whirlpool around the stanchions, you'd still go in. It'd be impossible to watch a little toddler screaming with terror in the water and just do nothing. You'd be in the water after the kid, risking your life, before you knew what you were doing.

That's what happened to me with Jacqui. I sat there nursing this big nude female (she was only a few pounds lighter than me), stroking her hair and patting her bottom, and I fell in love with her.

I found myself worrying and thinking about Jacqui all the time she wasn't with me. That's when you know you're in love with a woman, when you think about her when she's not with you. You can like any good-looking girl when you're with her. You look at her laughing, or you see her legs move, and you can feel really keen on her. Then, when she's been gone a few minutes, you never think of her till you see her again. Or you might feel sexy when you're on your own, and *then* you think of her. But when you think of her all the time, and she's not there, then you know you've fallen, boy.

I got all the other symptoms too. One is that you never seem to need any sleep. I'd work all day at taxiing, then drive to where Jacqui was just leaving the office she worked in. We'd come back to my place, have a really nice meal, then go to bed. We'd do all the usual things there, talk, have it off, play chess, eat dinner—till about four in the morning. Then we'd sleep till about six, wash and breakfast, and I'd take her to her office and head back to the taxi firm myself.

I think that's the most intense period anyone has in his whole life. The two of you seem to spend most of your time alone in the house together. You're never bored. You never have to think what you're going to do with the evening. You just feel loving and lovely all the time, even when you wake up in the morning. It's not so much that you have sex five or six times a day, it more or less goes on all the time. You spend four or five hours at a stretch just lying on the bed stroking one another, and talking about this and that and the other.

It's all lunacy, of course, love. A man should never fall in love with a woman, or a woman with a man. It's almost always a mistake. Two people should come together because they admire one another, because they find something decent and good in one another, not because their glands have gone crazy.

Falling in love is like any other really violent emotion that's going to get you in very big trouble some day, like anger or greed or jealousy or hate. Someone in love is mentally deficient. You might just as well blow your mind with LSD as fall in love. It's about as logical, and it'll do you about as much good in the long run.

Another of the lads we had once at the firm made that mistake just the year before. He fell in love with one of the little scrubbers and settled down with her and had a baby. Of course, it was all hopeless. She wanted what she called "the bright lights," which meant she wanted to sit around in the dark getting drunk and shooting drugs. This driver—Mike's his name—set her up in a nice little flat and was very decent to her, but she buggered off with the kid to live with some horrible little creep who was on heroin. He had the girl the same as himself six months later. The two of them looked like a pair of vampires, all eaten up with drugs, and the kid was all undersized and half-starved.

It all had a terrible effect on Mike. It aged him about forty years in twelve months. He was a strong, cheerful sort of lad before it started, but by the end his face was so lined he looked like an old man.

You'd think to yourself he could have broken loose, that he could have just forgotten it and left it all behind him. But he couldn't, of course. He was in love, and love makes people go insane.

The really mad thing was, I knew all the time what I was letting myself in for. I knew what Jacqui was. She called for me at the taxi office just after I'd met her, and the next day Chris said, "That's a right little drawers-dropper you've got yourself there, mate. Bet you're seeing some action."

I just laughed it off, said jealousy would get him nowhere. I made out she was just a casual thing with me, a one-night stand sort of thing. I knew I couldn't defend her. But it made my blood run cold. You can always rely on what other men say about your woman. Men have an instinct like that. Never for their own women though, only for other people's. When Chris saw Ilse one day he said, "Now that's what I call a beautiful girl. You want to hang on to her. She's miles too good for the likes of you, mind, but try not to let her find out."

So I did know what Jacqui was.

And what was even madder, knowing what she was, I decided having a baby by her would be a good idea. I can't imagine what I was thinking at the time. I'd never wanted babies by the decent girls I'd known. I'd never really fancied the idea of kids. Who would, when they see their friends and neighbors with them? Nothing puts you off kids faster than meeting people who've got them.

You go around to someone's house who's got kids and it's usually really messy and not nice at all. For a start, there's a permanent smell of crap everywhere when people have babies. The parents can't get away from it. Morning, noon, and night there's pottying to be done, and wet nappies all over the place.

Then, with a husband and a wife and a bunch of kids, everyone seems to be arguing all the time. You're never there five minutes before he's shouting at her, or she's glaring at him, or one of the kids has been belted and dragged off screaming upstairs.

And kids are always spilling things. You can't relax for a second or something's thrown over and smashed and there's a great big crying match started. They spoil everything. You might be having a really nice day out, at one of those lovely little tea shops out in the country, all sitting around the table. If it was just all grown-ups there you could have a really nice time, get an interesting conversation going, all that sort of thing.

But if you've got kids you might as well wave all that goodbye for at least half your life. You can't have anything decent. A little kid will break everything you've got. He'll scratch all the furniture and the walls. You might just as well have a chimp around the house as the average little kid.

I never wanted it. I thought it would bore me mental, having to sit in the house all day with a little kid and watch him pick his nose. "Once you let kids in the door," I always say to myself, "your peace of mind goes out the window." There's a sort of war going on inside you all the time when you have kids. On the one hand you want to keep all your money and things to yourself, and on the other the kid will kick your shins to get it off you.

You can see it any day of the week in town. There's the kid whining for an ice cream and the dad keeping his hands in his pocket. His face is a picture. He's all screwed up. He's thinking, "Damn the little bugger, he's not getting any more money out of me. I've got to slave to earn that stuff, then he thinks all he's got to do is yell his head off and it'll fly out of my pockets. I'll bash him if he doesn't shut up."

That's what he's *thinking*. But what he's *feeling* is completely different. He's a human grown-up and he's been conditioned for millions of years; when the kid opens his mouth and yells, you shove food down it. He knows bloody well ice cream isn't a food. He's not completely soft in the head. But what he *thinks* will never win over what he *feels*. It won't with you and me, neither. Nature's the winner every time, and the kid gets his ice cream. The dad might just as well have given in at the beginning and saved all the tantrums.

And another thing kids cost you, besides civilized life, they split you and your woman up. You might be getting on fine, having a really good sex life, and it'll all get ruined. You live with a woman because you love her and she loves you, then you have kids and you've got no more time for one another.

The trouble with women is, their first loyalty is to their kids, not to their feller. That's what most men don't ever cotton on to. They think they're sexy, or rugged, and their women can't do without them. But it's kids women can't do without, not men.

Most men think a woman should be loyal to *them*. They think they can get a woman up to the altar or in a registrar's office and make her swear an oath, then they think she's going to stick to that oath all her life.

What a hope! For a start, the average woman doesn't even know it's an oath she's taking. All *she* sees in the marriage is wearing a big white dress, and being the center of attention. It's her big day, the biggest day of her life. Oh, she might think she loves the guy the day she marries him. Maybe she *has* to think that. But if you want to see whether she loves the bloke or not, just see what happens if he comes between her and having kids.

Suppose he's the nicest guy in the world, he's generous, he doesn't nag her or hit her, he's fantastic around the house at fixing things and decorating things. And then, after he's married, he puts it to her like this, "Look, love, do you mind if we don't have any kids in our marriage? Oh, I know they can be cute and lovable, but they're very demanding and expensive. They'll wear you out and make an old woman out of you. We'll never have time to be with one another if we have kids. I'll be having to work all the hours God sends to pay for their clothes and bikes and things, and you'll be a slave over the kitchen sink. You'll get dishpan hands and wrinkles and I'll get middle-aged spread and go bald. Let's not do that. Let's just stay you and me. With the money we don't spend on children we'll have a beautiful home with every labor-saving convenience. We'll go to the theater at least once a week. We'll have six weeks' holiday every year. We'll go on a cruise at Christmas. We'll visit all the beautiful places in the world. I want you to be young and beautiful, educated and refined forever."

Now, how do you think a woman takes an offer like that? Does she think the guy's a living saint, that no finer man ever lived? Not on your life she doesn't! She thinks he's a pig, and she'll tell everyone he is, too. She'll say he's selfish and mean, that he's depriving her of a woman's greatest right, the right to be a drudge to a bunch of kids who think she's an old bag and can't grow up fast enough to get away from her. (Though she doesn't put it like that.)

She'll leave him. She'll go off with the biggest heel, just to have kids. He might booze, give her no money, hit her if his dinner's not ready. But, by God, he'll give her kids. He'll have her knocking them out one every year, and there she is happy and fulfilled. She spends her whole life wiping behinds and washing dishes. She's as thick as two short planks and about as refined as a privy, but she's a *real* woman.

No, any bloke who thinks a woman's ever going to be faithful to *him,* once she's got kids, has got another think coming.

But we all fall, don't we? When I first thought of having the kid, I was over the moon. It sounds stupid, I know, but I was high with my little self. You see other people with these big millstoney gangs of kids around their necks, and you wonder how they can be such mugs and what do they get out of it for spending their whole lives and every penny they've got bringing them up. And then you plan a kid of your own, and everything looks completely different. The idea seems really brilliant and you feel as happy as a Zulu with two clubs. You feel as though you've done something really clever. It comes to you like some marvelous discovery. You think to yourself, "What I always wanted to make my little word complete was a kid or two. Just give me one of those and I'll never need anything else to cheer me up in life."

I was so bowled over when Jacqui suggested it to me that she thought she'd upset me. But the reason I couldn't talk was I felt so happy about the idea. I felt as though I was a bottle and someone had filled me up with fizzy lemonade. I couldn't wait to get Jacqui back home and get started. (I was just dropping her off at her own house in the early hours.)

We'd already had it away about six times that evening, in between chess moves, but I couldn't wait to get started doing it with the definite idea of having a baby.

I discovered that was a whole new thing altogether. Having sex with a girl you like can be a very pleasant experience, but when you're doing it to have a baby, deliberately, it's something else altogether. It gives you a whole new outlook on life. You realize that these little guys you see around with bunches of kids are really dark horses. They look like nothing on earth, yet when you think of the fun they've had churning them out, you realize they've known real joy. It's hard to believe when you look at them, but they've experienced the best thing life has to offer.

I don't care what anyone says, making a child, making a child when you *want* to make a child, is the finest thing there could ever possibly be in life.

I could see my own little kid long before he was born. I even knew it was going to be a him and not a her. I seemed to be in touch with him, as though he was part of my mind before he went into his mother's body. I always saw him as a tiny little fetus, inside a big sort of soap bubble. I couldn't see his eyes, he had them shut. And he didn't talk to me, because he was only a little baby. But I could *feel* for him, if you know what I mean. I could think of him and love him just as though he'd been born and was lying in a crib and I was looking at him.

I couldn't do enough for Jacqui, for having him. The first thing I did was buy a wedding ring, I wasn't having anyone calling my little boy a bastard.

I didn't buy an engagement ring, I've always thought they were silly things, and what's getting engaged got to do with getting married anyway? You get these young girls flashing around their tiny little diamond, and it just looks silly. A wedding ring's solid and rich, with a beautiful warm color, like a marriage should be, but an engagement ring's cold and glassy and doesn't say anything to me at all.

I couldn't believe how much fun I got out of buying that ring. You see other blokes and girls standing at the shop window looking at the trays, and they're so terrifically serious about it all, and you think "What a waste of time. Why don't they just live together?"

But when you come to buy a ring for your own girl, it feels like magic. It was a really freezing cold day when we went to get it, but I felt all warm inside, and when it came to paying for it I couldn't get the money out fast enough. I felt really proud of Jacqui, standing there. She looked so beautiful (to me anyway), and I kept imagining I could see signs of the pregnancy already: Her breasts getting bigger, and her face going smooth and pink, and all that sort of stuff.

I felt really happy and contented and beautiful about it all. I felt like a married man, soon to be a father, and it felt like the best thing in the world. Jacqui was so sweet and nice it was incredible. She wouldn't wear the ring until we'd gone around to a little back street engraver and had my name cut inside it. Then she asked me to put it on her ring finger, and when I did that she gave me a long kiss, with her lips all warm in spite of the cold, and I felt the happiest man alive.

Chapter

2

And then, when Jacqui had me nice and safely tied down, ring and all, she started shoveling it on me, she started treating me like dirt.

The first thing she did was take me around to her father's. That was a real sickener. Her old man was one of those little London poufs you see in the thousands up around West One and Two. They always have some kind of uniform so they know each other. One time it was suede; suede shoes and jacket, with a colored silk cravat around their necks. This time I was talking about, it was the butch look, tight jeans with a black leather jacket. And those glasses that have a blue tinge to them. Just to be in the fashion, Jacqui's old feller would have his shades on at nighttime when the light was so bad you could hardly see a thing.

He started drinking in the evening, and the next thing he was off. He started going up and down the room with a glass in his hand telling me what a big shot he was. If he was to be believed, he'd been involved in all kinds of bank and check frauds. He had a mate who had learned to fiddle those automatic tellers you get outside banks, and the two of them had gone around collecting twenty-five pounds a time before the banks changed the system. Then there was this other fiddle they'd done up in the Midlands, opening accounts in every bank in town, then overdrawing at each place and running with the loot.

My blood was running cold while I was listening to this. I've always hated crooks trying to get a free ride. They want other people to provide the buses and the taxis of life, and they steal a lift and pay nothing. They're like fleas and lice and tapeworms, just parasites. Every few weeks you get one of them trying it on with taxi rides, they get you to drive them to the middle of nowhere at twelve at night, and then they try and get out of paying. They're scum.

And this one was going to be my little boy's grandfather. Even if he was a bloody little liar, it was a terrible way to be talking in front of your family. What kind of outlook would your kids get on life if they thought all the people around them were there just to be diddled? No wonder Jacqui was practically a whore, with that creep as her dad.

He kept talking about ordinary people as "the harmless millions." Well it's the harmless millions make the world go around, the farmers and the engineers and the shop-keepers. It's certainly not the poufs and the bents up in the West End who do it. It's the horse that does the running, not the parasites on its ass.

But there was worse to come. Jacqui's dad and his second wife went out about eight in the evening and me and Jacqui were left baby-sitting.

We were sitting in the house quietly about nine o'clock, Jacqui's little half sister was asleep in her bed, when the phone rang and Jacqui answered it. She spoke to someone for a minute, then hung up and came over to where I was sitting on the couch.

"That was an old friend of mine," she said. "He wants me to translate a letter from French for him and he'll take me to dinner at Frère Jacques while I do it."

"Well," I thought, "tell him you can't go, you're booked from now on. You're going to be a mother and . . ."

But the next thing I knew she was coming downstairs with an evening dress on and she was rouging her cheeks and mascaraing her eyes in front of the mirror.

"Where are you going?" I asked her. I was really stupid just around then.

"Oh, I must go out and do this letter for him," she said. "He's an old friend, and he's off to South Africa tomorrow. He won't be back for two years. And I love eating at Frère Jacques."

I knew she was lying. The dress she had on hardly held

her boobs in, and she had this sort of glitter in her eyes. I'd been feeling all warm and peaceful before that, but now I suddenly felt icy cold and the night was really miserable.

I shouldn't have let her go. When I heard the feller's taxi at the door I should have gone downstairs and told him she wasn't going.

I thought afterward I should have gone down to the door and told him we were getting married.

Boy, would he have laughed though! He'd have found that hilarious, me being all dignified about getting engaged to an old tail.

What I did instead, I got Jacqui to promise she'd be faithful. What an idiot! I got her to wear her gold wedding ring, and when she had it on and she was twisting it around her finger I said, "You'll be faithful, won't you? You'll remember me and the baby?" And she promised faithfully she would.

I'll bet she did! As far as the bottoms of the stairs. I'll bet she had the ring off and in her purse before she got to the front door.

Either that or the other bloke got a kick out of banging someone's fresh new fiancée who had just started a baby.

But what can a bloke do with a randy woman? He can't watch her all day and night. If you've got a wandering girl friend you're onto a loser. I sat down on the couch with my heart like lead. I would have gone off, but I couldn't just leave the little girl alone in the house. Midnight came, and Jacqui still wasn't back. One o'clock, and I must have fallen asleep.

She finally came in about two in the morning. I was

asleep on the couch, and she woke me up. It was like waking up into a nightmare. We sat down at the table while I was trying to get my eyes open. You know what it's like when someone wakes you at two in the morning, you feel as though your head's in the next room. Jacqui sat looking at me and twisting the wedding ring on her finger.

"Well?" I said finally. I was wishing I was an animal, so I could just forget what she'd been up to.

She sort of filled me in on what I'd been missing, not having gone with her, and been asleep and all. She'd gone out with this bloke, had a meal, then gone back to his place for a friendly screw. "But it's OK," she said, "we didn't go all the way, we just sort of went in and out without doing anything."

I was to get used to that "sort of" with her. Everything was always "sort of" with Jacqui, as though she could never be positive about anything. Especially about her screwing with other blokes. She always "sort of" didn't like them, or "sort of" got a pleasure out of it.

She got me into the same habit. I've never been able to stop myself "sort of-ing" ever since.

It was all terrible, of course. She'd no sooner got me to try and start a baby with her, then she went off shafting with this bloke she said she didn't even like. I should have got rid of her then. I should have just gone off and not looked back. It seems mad now, staying. You do some really stupid things in your life, but hanging around a screw-happy woman must be about the worst.

Around about this time I was reading Somerset

Maugham's book *Of Human Bondage*. You do a lot of reading in taxi work, while you're waiting for fares. Most of the other lads just read newspapers and magazines and stuff, but I try to learn things. I buy a lot of magazines every week and read about gardening and house repair. And every now and then I find a good book, a novel, and have a really interesting read.

Well, in this book, practically the same thing happened to me happened to Somerset Maugham. He fell in love with this stupid bird who worked in a café as a waitress, and she put him through the hoop as well. She practically destroyed him. She spent all his money, so he had to give up trying to be a doctor and take this really deadly job working in a department store. Then she ran off with this really seedy guy who ditched her, so she ran back to poor old Somerset. Then, when he let her live in his flat, she slashed and broke every single thing in it. She didn't just go mad and smash things, she waited till he was out for the day, then spent the whole eight hours really meticulously destroying every single thing he had in the whole place. It was a terrific book, *Of Human Bondage*. All the time Jacqui was wrecking me, I thought of that story.

"You're not alone," I kept saying to myself, "there's lots of other poor guys suffer the same way at the hands of women."

It was later that same night I had the first of my nightmares about her. We were climbing this mountain together, me and Jacqui. We were rushing up it, trying to get away from something. I was half carrying her. To tell the truth, I was half-frantic trying to protect her. Something was after us, I didn't know what it was, but it was something made me feel all sick and terrified, so I was shaking and panting and crying as we scrambled up these great big slabs of rock miles high in the sky. The thing that was chasing us was after Jacqui. It was trying to get her, and I was going frantic trying to keep it away from her. I felt if I could only get her over the top of the mountain we'd be safe. She was hurrying, too, but she was sort of weak and helpless, and I was having to lift her and push her all the time.

And then this thing caught up with us. The dream went mad just there. One minute, we were miles up the mountain, and the next, there was this bloke standing next to us where there wasn't even anything to stand on, just a terrific great drop down to nowhere, and this gigantic figure hanging in the sky, as big as two houses, with a tommy gun as long as a car. He was dressed like a Nazi during the war, and he had this tommy gun in his hand pointed at Jacqui, and I realized he was going to shoot her.

I went frantic. I was shouting "No—no!" and trying to scramble across the rocks to get between him and Jacqui, I was trying to throw myself in the way of the bullet. I thought if I could stop the bullet with my chest Jacqui would be OK. It was stupid, of course. I realized, when I woke up, that if he'd killed me Jacqui would have been completely helpless, but I wasn't thinking that at the time. All I was trying to do was make sure the bullet hit me and not her. I could see the bullet as clear as anything, this big ugly lead thing the size of a bucket, and I was trying to make myself wider to catch it.

And then I woke up and I was on the couch in the living room and I was drenched in sweat and shivering like mad. I was feeling more scared and sick than I'd ever felt in my life before. If I'd known what was ahead of me, it probably would have finished me off there and then.

The next day we went walking in the park, and Jacqui started to tell me all about the bloke from the night before. She'd been having sex with him for about a year or so. She didn't like him much, she said she found him "drippy," but he bought her expensive meals, and in exchange she went back to his flat and had sex with him.

When I said that made her a prostitute, she looked all worried.

"Does it?" she said. "Surely it doesn't? I mean, I don't take money for it. I only sort of get a meal."

She was looking really frightened and upset. I found out why that same night, when she told me her life story. Jacqui was really terrified of going over the brink.

You often get that, if someone's on the edge of something really evil, if they're going alcoholic, or getting very bitter about something, or starting to give their wife a bad time, they hate to be told it. They're like someone who's caught cancer, they'd rather not be given the bad news. Jacqui was like that about becoming a pro, though I didn't know it at the time.

"Of course it does," I said, not realizing the effect it was going to have on her. "Prostitution is selling sex—whatever you sell it for."

Then she said something that really worried and frightened me. Her face went all dark and sullen, like in her picture when she was a teenager, and she sort of growled out, "I suppose that's all I'm good for, being a slut, I'm so fat and ugly."

She looked really full of hate for herself.

I tried to pull her around, telling her she was talking stupid, that she was a lovely girl. I put my arm around her as we walked along, to comfort her.

But suddenly, she went berserk. She started behaving like a lunatic. She dived down on the ground and started rolling around screaming. She was actually shouting, "I'm fat! I'm ugly! I'm a slut!"

It's a good thing it was early on a Sunday morning and no one was around. It took me a quarter of an hour to calm her down. Every time I tried to pick her up she just made herself go limp, like little children do. It was a winter's day, and the turf was wet and full of worm casts, but she kept falling down on it and rolling about and screaming. She was wearing one of those pink rubberized macs, and it and her hands and the knees of her jeans were all wet and dirty.

And all the time a voice kept saying to me, "This woman's a lunatic. She's goig to be very big trouble for you. If you're a clever lad you'll just leave her lying in the dirt and walk away. If you don't, you'll be very sorry."

They say love's blind. Well, it's deaf and dumb and mentally deficient as well.

You know what I thought, you know how stupid I was? I thought I could help her. I thought I could get her to reform. One of the surest things in life is that a leopard doesn't change his spots.

You know the story about the guy who feels sorry for the worm he finds swimming around in the cowpat. "Poor little thing," he thinks, "what a terrible way to live, how unhappy you must be."

So he takes the worm home, washes it in scented water, powders its little bottom, and sits it on a silk cushion. "There," he says, "you're much happier now, aren't you?"

But do you think the worm's happy? Not on your life he isn't! As soon as ever the bloke's back's turned he's off the cushion and cantering down the road toward his cowpat. The moral of this story is, if you find a guy living in the dirt, a druggie, a drunk, or even just a slob, leave him there. He probably belongs there and won't be happy anywhere else.

You get dozens of social cripples like that in your taxi, but it's suicide to try and help them.

One time I picked up a woman who was a drug addict, and she gave me a terrible day. For one thing, she didn't know where she wanted to go. She had me driving around town, out in the country, everywhere. She kept weeping all over the place, which made me feel sorry for her, and then when she thought my back was turned, she'd be popping all these tablets, great big handfuls of them, and crunching them up like candies. I said I'd take her to a hospital, or a police station, but she had hysterics and said she'd kill herself if I did that.

Then she started getting sexy. She kept saying things like, "Do you know what color knickers I've got on?" And then she'd go into fits of giggling and say she wasn't wearing any.

Then she'd do the husky voice and say, "I like to make love, naked, on a double bed."

In the end, I passed a couple of policewomen, dropped this lunatic woman off on the pavement, then reported it to the policewomen before driving off.

It was the only thing to do.

This wasn't just one bit of bad luck she was having, this was the end product of years of her life. There were years of building up to what she was doing now.

The same goes for someone like Jacqui, who's screwing around. She didn't *have* to do it. No one was holding a gun to her head. She had the whole big beautiful world all around her, and she was free to pick any bit of it she wanted. If she chose the bit between two sheets with some grotty little guy she didn't even like, then that told you a lot about her.

But instead of leaving Jacqui where she belonged (in the dirt), I took her home with me and let her cry on my shoulder. The Billy Graham of the taxi service. The story she told me would have made your hair stand on end.

Ever since Jacqui was a little girl, her dad had been turning her into a crook. When the law was on to that two-bit criminal, he'd use his kids as an alibi. He'd get

Jacqui to swear to the cops he'd been with her all day. She was only about nine, and he'd coach her in all these lies. The poor kid grew up not knowing what the truth was.

Then there was her mother. The family used to spend months in Naples on the money they made on crooked deals. Jacqui's mother was mad about sailors. She used to take her two little girls walking around town trying to pick up sailors from the NATO ships in the harbor. She was always getting herself in big trouble with all kinds of drunks and psychopaths. One time she was knifed. Another time some guy pushed her out of a taxi doing about forty miles an hour. She was always tormenting her husband. She'd be in the back of taxis necking and groping like mad with some bloke while her husband was there. Then they'd jump out, and leave Jacqui's dad to pay the fare.

Jacqui's mother hated Jacqui's father. It seems he wasn't only a crook, but he was bent too. When they lived together he used to have orgies with his queer mates where they wore makeup and ran around naked, goosing one another. That's what drove her promiscuous. Before she got married she was a very decent girl, but her husband disgusted her so much it changed her whole character.

The family history sounded like the plot of a blue movie. Jacqui told me her sister went on drugs when she was thirteen, then took to prostituting herself to get money for them. She used to come home from school, change out of her school uniform, then go up Park Lane soliciting all the dirty old perverts who hang around up there. She was only fourteen years of age when she started that. She had the pox by the time she was fifteen.

Jacqui said that with all the turmoil in the family she used to get these terrible black depressions. She had this feeling she was being sucked down into all this evil. She even turned to religion to protect herself. She joined the Jehovah's Witnesses, but got herself seduced by a guy when she was taking *The Watchtower* around to his house. After that she just went mad. She'd do it with anyone. She didn't enjoy it, but she didn't seem able to resist. She tried to take her life twice, once by cutting her wrist with a razor blade, and a second time by taking an overdose.

I sat there listening to all this and my mind was ticking over twenty to the dozen. What I was thinking was, "I should get the hell out of this fix." I knew that. I should have just got rid of Jacqui and not even looked back. Who would have blamed me in the circumstances?

But I kept feeling sorry for her. And I kept thinking of the baby, too. If *I* didn't stick around to protect him, what sort of life would he have? He'd probably go and live with his bent grandad and grow up a crook. Either that or his mother would shack up with some really squalid little bugger who'd corrupt and molest him.

I was in a really big quandary. So instead of doing the right thing, ditching Jacqui, I put my arms around her and dried her face. I told her not to worry, to put it all behind her. I told her I'd just forget it all, that as far as I was concerned she was a pure young girl.

I must have looked a right idiot to her. I used to look

71

back on that later and wonder how I could ever be so weak in the head. But the thing was, Jacqui was being so contrite. She was swearing she'd reform. She said the baby would change her whole life, that she'd become different for his sake, a loving mother, and all the rest of it. I believed her. I forgot all about the little worm, and I believed her. I thought a miracle might happen, if you could imagine I was that daft.

And what made it even worse, I had another chance to get away. Jacqui phoned me about the end of November and said she wasn't pregnant, that she'd just had a period.

I should have thought "Great," and taken off like a little bird. If I'd had only half a brain, I'd have done just that. I must have been mental to stick around when the door had just been opened.

But I didn't fly the coop. The truth is, I felt choked when I realized I wasn't going to be a father. I felt really unhappy and lost when Jacqui told me she wasn't having my kid. I only cheered up when she suggested we try again.

Of course, she was really sweet during that time, while I got her pregnant again, this time for certain. Then with the baby safely on the way, she went mad again. She said one night she had to go around to her mother's, and that started everything off again, the worries, the nightmares, the lot.

Her mother lived in one of those gloomy streets in Earl's Court where the houses are all let out in millions of little flats with rows of bells on each front door. Jacqui's mother lived on the third floor with this vicious little drunk called Carl and Jacqui's sister Louise, who was on the game.

My Christ, the place was a shambles. Everyone just sat around all day and drank cheap Italian red. Even the flies were drunk in there. They drank the wine slops off the table then staggered around all over the place, walking on your face and doing loop-the-loops in midair. I asked to use the loo and wished I hadn't. It was like something out of the Middle Ages. You could have cleaned it with a pneumatic drill.

Back from the loo, I saw another bloke had turned up, a little bald guy with pebble glasses and a grubby trench-coat. He looked like the original Hyde Park flasher. He was one of Louise's customers and they disappeared off for a screw together.

Then we all settled down for a pleasant evening's chat. That seemed to be entirely about who was banging who and who was bent. I went in the kitchen to wash a couple of glasses (I didn't want me and Jacqui catching the clap off the ones that were there), and it was like somewhere you'd boil up pigswill, if you had a bunch of pigs who weren't too choosy.

After about an hour, this horrible little drunk, Carl, started groping Jacqui right in front of me. The thing that sickened me was she made no attempt to stop it. She was supposed to be reforming, she was supposed to be having a baby, yet she let this pukey little drunk drag her on his knee and start trying to force her legs apart so he could get his hand on her fanny. He was living with her mother, yet her mother did nothing to stop it. Why *I* didn't do anything to stop it I can't imagine, I seemed sort of paralyzed.

You often get that with blokes, though. Their woman starts behaving like a lunatic and they do nothing at all about it. Before it or after it you think things like "I'd slap her around," or "I'd talk her out of it." But when it happens you just stand around like a dick. Some guy's groping your woman, the woman who's going to have your kid, right in front of you, and you don't raise a finger to try and stop him.

I think it's only if the woman resists you can do anything.

That really depressed me afterward. I thought, "I can't be on Jacqui's tail *all* the time, I can't be doing *all* the thinking for her, yet every time I leave her alone she gets into something sordid."

Back into the cowpat.

But what made me most depressed of all was afterward she said it didn't matter. She said it just like that, "It doesn't matter. It isn't important." She had a sort of glazed look in her eye while she said it. That really worried me rigid.

It reminded me of those suicidal drunks that get all smashed up, and their suits get ruined with vomit and blood, but it doesn't worry them.

They've got no self-respect. A normal girl, if some drunken pig tried to grope her in company, she'd go berserk. She'd whack him one, or she'd start a tremendous row. But all Jacqui could say was, "It doesn't matter." It was like a death wish.

I wanted to break loose, but I was like torn in half. On the one hand I hated the way Jacqui was carrying on, but on the other hand I was madly in love with the baby.

I did the only thing I could. I tried to forget the squalid side of things and concentrate on my little son.

I was really looking forward to him coming into the world. I knew I was going to look just as stupid as all the other guys at work, flashing pictures no one else was interested in: the baby in his little bed and the baby on his pot, and all the rest of it. But I didn't mind. I didn't care about being stupid, I was just high on the thought of him being born.

I made all sorts of plans around the house. I fitted out the box room alongside my own bedroom just for him. I bought a teddy bear and a little llama for him and hung cute little pictures on the wall. I found myself going into toy shops and winding up all the little clocks and trains and things they've got there. I could've got myself arrested, peeking in all the babies' prams and going "ootchy-coo" to them all.

I had really beautiful thoughts about him.

I had visions of myself piggybacking him up to bed at night, with him laughing and me rolling him onto the bed, tucking him up and reading him a bedtime story.

I even built him a little swimming pool in the garden. I knew he'd be about three before he could use it, but I went out there and spent weeks of my spare time digging the pit and lining it with bricks and cementing it. I spent a whole week trying to decide how deep it should be. I did everything but go around measuring little kids to see how high off the ground their chests come. Finally, I dug one end a foot deep and sloped it to four the other. That way he could use it from when he was a toddler to when he was nearly grown up.

It was freezing weather all the time I was digging it, but I kept thinking of him splashing around in it in the hot sun, and I didn't mind the cold a bit.

I realized then it's stupid not to give things to your kids. What else have you got besides them? They might be jammy and noisy, but they're a million times better than no kids at all. What's the good of money in the bank if your life's empty? Much better to have a houseful of kids and be happy, even if you're running to the pawnshop with the bedclothes and you haven't got two pennies to jingle together, like in the old days.

What's the good of having a sports car and going on holidays to the Med? You see these guys with sports cars, they all turn them in for a wife and kids eventually. Except the odd one or two. And they just look stupider and stupider as they get older, and they're still driving around in an MGB with the silk scarf around their wrinkled old neck and all their hair falling out. You wonder who they think they're kidding.

And as for holidays in the Med, they're not all they're cracked up to be. It's usually too hot, for one thing, and you get the face burned off you. It's too hot to walk anywhere, and if you get in a car it's like stepping into a baker's oven. You could burn your hands on the steering wheel. So you've got to spend your time in the hotel pool, along with about a million other people, all shrieking and splashing water around. Or you can try the sea. That's spooky as hell. Every time you go more than knee-deep you keep thinking of sharks and octopuses. And just at the end of the beach there's someone's sewer outlet. It's bad enough when it's your own people's, but when it's Italian and Spanish, I go right off it. I don't even like garlic.

Thinking of the baby coming was a hundred times better than anything I'd ever done before, especially as Jacqui started to come and stay at the house more often. I really enjoyed that.

The only snag was, living with her was like living with a mule. The way she did things, she got out of bed in the morning and shoved the duvet on the floor, and that's where it stayed all day as far as she was concerned. Then she went in the bathroom and splashed around and dumped the wet towel on the floor. Then she spent hours in front of the mirror picking at her eyes and shoving makeup on. She wouldn't eat breakfast in case it made her fat, then she'd get ravenous later on in the day and pig out. Then she'd hang around the house filing her nails and saying, "There's nothing to do here, I'm so *bored*."

If I suggested she help me make the bed or clean up the bathroom she'd say, "Oh, how bourgeois, cleaning up your little house."

And in the end she'd sit down in front of the television and watch everything that came on, all the rubbish, all the serials, all the contests, the pop scene, all the garbage you could imagine.

She was a total drag at mealtimes. One time I'd cook a

beautiful dinner, and she'd refuse to eat anything and just sit there sipping a glass of water and calling me a pig if *I* ate anything. Then the next day she'd wolf a whole roast chicken or a leg of lamb and make herself sick, and I'd have to nurse her through a gigantic bellyache. She got terrible breath through doing that, and I had to lie beside her all night and smell the stink of her.

Another time I bought five pounds of grapes and she tried to eat the whole lot in one go. I had to hide them from her to stop her. Then she was sick all night with pains in the stomach, and I thought she was going to miscarry, and I hauled some poor doctor out at three in the morning to see her.

I did try to lift her, I did try to get her brain working.

I tried to get her reading. Old Mr. Williamson's study room was full of really interesting books, but she couldn't be bothered. If she looked inside a book, her face used to go totally blank. Right away, the instant she looked at the page. It was as though her brain was programmed to switch off the second you confronted it with anything intelligent, in case it broke down through overload.

She wasn't even interested in her own pregnancy. I bought her a big book on childbirth, with lots of pictures and explanations of what it was all about, what to do for the best and all that, and she just dumped it in with the kitchen rubbish.

I had it all nicely done up for her, but when she unwrapped it she just said, "Did I ask for this?"

"Well, no, but I thought it might be useful . . ."

"Oh, you did, did you?" she said, and went to the sink and dumped it in the pedal bin underneath.

I could have cried when I thought of the difference between her and Ilse. Ilse was lovely around the house. In the summer we'd both be up at six in the morning. You know how beautiful it is then in the garden on a bright day, you feel tremendously peaceful and good, and by the time nine in the evening comes, you're all drowsy and loving.

We'd work all day, just pottering at little jobs, and reading. Everything Ilse touched she made beautiful. She had flowers blooming everywhere.

About the only thing that seemed to interest Jacqui (besides fiddling with her face), was having sex. I didn't want to have sex, I was worried about the baby. I kept thinking of him inside her and thought how dangerous it would be lying on her and maybe crushing him.

She thought I was stupid, of course.

"Don't be stupid," she'd say, "of course you won't hurt the baby." And the next thing she'd have me at it. I didn't like to think of her wanting it, and me being mean with it, so I'd go ahead and do a really nice job for her. Everything worked all right, but I never got over worrying about hurting the child. I'd sort of do it on the tips of my elbows and my toes, so as not to put any pressure on him.

But it never seemed right having sex when the baby was already started. We'd had sex to get him going, and once we'd done that there didn't seem any point doing it anymore. Animals have more sense than human beings about that. I still felt loving toward Jacqui. I'd put my arms around her a lot, and I was always buying her things, but I didn't want to go all the way.

She got more and more depressing to live with. I really could have wept sometimes. She made the house sort of violent. She got me to buy a portable TV set, then set it up in the bedroom so she could sit and watch in bed. The bedroom used to be a little sanctuary, and she turned it into a noisy picture house.

Why I went on doing it, I'll never know. I think men are just lunatics where women are concerned. They can be sensible in anything else but that. I think it's part of nature. If you get a female pregnant, you've got this instinct to stick with her. Even animals do it. You watch the birds in the garden, and the blackbird will never go far from the nest while the hen's sitting.

I even had another golden opportunity to get rid of her, but I blew it like all the others.

She got this mad idea of going away to be a mother's helper. She applied for a job without telling me anything, then announced she had to go to Shropshire for a month, being a mother's helper to three posh little kids.

I should have been over the moon. In a month I could have got rid of her. I could have found a decent girl and had her installed if Jacqui had tried to come back. She could have had an abortion and gone her little way, and I'd have forgotten all about her, and then at least she wouldn't be dead. She'd only have been walking the streets, but at least she would have had her life.

But somehow I just couldn't get rid of her. It worried the life out of me. It made me all anxious and nervous to be separated from her, I couldn't seem to eat or sleep or anything. I asked her not to go. I told her to tell the woman to get someone else. It wasn't as if she was a friend. She just wanted someone to do all the boring work with her kids, so she could get away from them herself. I said you didn't owe anyone anything in a situation like that, if someone's just paying you to do their drudgery. I said she was pregnant, that she had a duty to the child, to me, to herself. . . .

I might as well have talked to the wall. It ended up with me driving her all the way there myself, to this little place on the other side of Wolverhampton. It was one of those big manor farmhouse places like you see on television. The woman was kind of cool and snotty. I think she fancied herself as a society beauty or something. She had these three dingy-looking little kids who were always stuck up on ponies. Her husband only came home for Christmas with them, the rest of the time he lived out in Ceylon with native women. When you saw the setup, you didn't blame him.

The whole business cost me about three times as much as Jacqui earned on the job. It ended up with me phoning her every night for two hours, long distance, and altogether I made three trips in the car to see her, once to drop her there, once to take her some extra clothes, and the third time to drive her to Snowdonia for a day out.

Then when she came back again, a month later, she'd really got the devil in her. I thought she'd been bad before, but now she'd gone really evil. She'd seen the rich way the people in her manor house lived, and she fancied the same thing for herself. The people she'd been staying with had got their money by farming and working hard, but that didn't seem to occur to Jacqui. I mean, she didn't suggest we buy a small holding, slave twenty-five hours a day, and work our way up.

All she could think of was some grotty, pimpy way of getting to the same place, the sort of thing her dad had taught her.

She reckoned she had a product to sell, and she could make a living out of it.

She was right, really. A good-looking girl of eighteen or nineteen can wheedle the money out of a man's wallet with no trouble at all.

She started going on about how she'd like to get on the game, do it professionally like a business.

"It's so easy," she kept saying, "you make big money for doing absolutely nothing, just lying there."

She told me about these clubs in town you could go to where you picked up men. The girls wore very sexy clothes and drank with the customers, then if the customer fancied the girl he took her back to his hotel or flat or whatever, and she got the equivalent of a normal week's wages for an hour's work.

Normally, when you hear of that sort of thing, it's just a big joke. You get movies showing it as a sort of fun thing even, much better than just being married and having kids. But when your own woman starts thinking of doing it, you realize just how sick it really is. It's like a nightmare. Jacqui told me about it one evening, and it was just like one of those horror films where Evil or the Menace, or whatever it is, comes into the house. One minute the house is all warm and normal, and the next there's a sort of horrific mist comes under the doors, or there's a darkness and all the lights start going out. That's how you feel when *your* woman, carrying *your* baby, talks about going streetwalking.

It's all right for the guys with the money to go around the clubs shagging the girls. They have a good time. But I don't suppose it would ever occur to them there's probably a tragedy behind every girl they screw. There's either some pimp threatening to give her a razor across the face if she doesn't bring home the money, or he's got her hooked on hard drugs and threatens to cut off the supply if she doesn't get horizontal double quick. Either that or there's family, like me, sitting at home grieving because the girl's too mentally retarded to know any better.

In all those little houses, miles from the night spots, there's parents worried about their daughters, kids grieving their little hearts out for their mothers, and blokes like me, family men, seeing all their plans for a decent life in ruins. Unless they do something about it.

Chapter

3

Sometimes I get the idea Jacqui must have been mad. I mean, really insane, the way doctors mean it. She seemed to have some kind of death wish. That time I took her up to Shropshire, she nearly killed the two of us. She yanked this pullover over my head when we were doing seventy. It was one of those knobbly wool sweaters that fell to pieces in about twelve months. They were right in the fashion then. Jacqui unwrapped the thing in the car. It was my Christmas present from her. (She'd got the money for it from me the week before.) She held it up and asked me if I liked it.

"Do you like it?" she said. And then, "Let's see if it fits." Without any warning she yanked it over my head to try it on. I think she must have been insane. We were in real danger for a second or two. It's a bit tricky doing a mile a minute when you can't see where you're going because someone's wrapped a bloody pullover around your head.

I thought some desperate things myself, I felt so trapped. A lunatic woman like that cons you into getting her pregnant, and then you're stuck with her. Once you've had a kid by someone, you can't ever really cut them out of your life. You're trying to live decently and sensibly, and they're all the time doing insane things.

I thought a good old-fashioned belting might be the answer. You know how you feel when your woman's being stupid and won't listen to you, you feel like battering her. You think if she had a good punching it might bring her to her senses. Many a time I felt my fists curling up at the thought of it. I often think now that's what I should have done. If I'd beaten her up it might have woken her up. Perhaps some women just need regular hidings. Maybe they act stupidly because they *want* you to hit them.

But women have made the rules about that, too. A woman can use any dirty trick in the book, but you're not allowed to hit her. That's "mean" and cowardly," and "taking advantage of your physical strength." The woman can nag her feller, burn his dinner, waste his money, shag with the milkman, but *he's* not supposed to retaliate. He's not allowed to smack her in the teeth or land her one around the ear. No one can touch *her* for any of the dirty tricks *she* plays. Just let the husband lash out and he can find himself inside. He can be a really decent, nice guy, and she can be a raving whore, but he'll still find himself in court if he gives her a black eye.

So instead of hitting her, I tried pleading with her. Nothing looks dopier than a bloke pleading with a woman. She almost always despises him for it.

"Don't go prostituting," I said, "I'll *give* you that much a week if you don't do it."

"You?" she said. She was sort of jeering at me. "Where would *you* get big money to give me?"

"Don't worry," I said. "I'll get it. I'll work overtime. I'll get it somehow if only you don't go joining that club."

She seemed to think that was hilarious.

"So you'll run around all night in your little taxi just to stop me making a big of money on the side?" she said.

"Yes," I said, "I'll do that. I'll take out a second mortgage on the house if that'll keep you happy."

I would have, too. The thought of my little boy trapped inside Jacqui, and her talking about going prostituting, was driving me crazy. I kept having these horrific visions of him inside her womb and some dirty old pervert lying on him and sticking his horrible diseased old cock in my child's only home. I'd have sacrificed my house and lived in a room somewhere to prevent that.

I don't think I was overreacting. It wasn't that I expected Jacqui to be faithful or anything, or just only think of me. A man's very bigheaded if he expects his woman to be like that. Any normal woman's got a whole lot of lovers in her head, besides the feller she's sleeping with. You meet women who've got pictures of Robert Redford, Gary Cooper, and the like all over the house, and they're always mooning over them, even when the husband's there. I knew a bird had Paul Newman in the lavatory. Even when you're having it off with a woman you're never sure it's *you* she's thinking of.

I took a couple home once, and she had Elvis Presley, six by four, right across one wall of the kitchen. They called me in for a drink, then started rowing about it. He said he was going to tear it down and she said, "Leave him up there, he's a bloody sight nicer looking than you are!"

To her husband! He's only going out working every day of his life to keep her, and she insults him like that. It was probably *his* money she bought the picture with.

But prostitution? That's another thing altogether. When you think what it means to be a prostitute it makes you feel sick to death. You've got to let yourself be mauled all over by just anyone who fancies it and can pay you the money. And you'll almost certainly get the very worst of guys wanting it, all the little bent fellers, the smellies, the drunks, the sort of blokes you squirm just talking to. You've not only got to talk to them all, you've got to go to bed with them. It made me feel like being sick just thinking about it.

A woman's either got to be mad to be a prostitute, or it drives her insane doing it. If you're taxiing late at night and you see a woman screaming and effing or lying on the pavement, you can bet your life she's an old tail.

Jacqui's sister was a typical-enough example. She was one of the most screwed-up and unhappy people I ever met in all my life. I had a couple of long talks with her while I was at her mother's. The stories she told would make your hair stand on end. She started being a prostitute because she got hooked on drugs when she was thirteen years of age. She was terrifically unhappy. She was always trying to commit suicide. She couldn't bear to see daylight, it made her feel so chronic, so she tried to sleep all day by getting blind drunk or drugging herself. She couldn't stand the silence, either, so she had this radio by the bed all the time blasting out. Her bedroom was hellish. There was all this litter and muddle and dirt and these bloody awful noises the pop singers make, and in the middle of it all was Louise sprawled on the bed in a sort of coma. She hated her customers, the men who used her. She said she'd like to kill them all, but as she couldn't kill them she always tried to give them all a dose. (She had all kinds of venereal diseases.) She said it was a pity penicillin had been invented, so now they could be cured. She said they should all suffer like mad and die in agony.

And Jacqui was heading the same way. She was young, she had her health and strength, she had the whole world to enjoy. There were all sorts of beautiful things around her, the sun, the fresh air, trees, flowers, good books, yet all she could think to do was have really squalid little shack-ups with perverted blokes.

She never went out anywhere except at night. She just sat around the house all day messing about with her body and squealing if you let a breath of fresh air in.

And she started having the same effect on me. She sort of dragged me down. After a couple of months knowing her, all I could see in the world was pimps and prostitutes and stuff. I found it hard to think of all the nice things I'd enjoyed before her. I found it difficult working around the house or digging in the garden. I'd wake up in the morning, and everything would look dull and dingy, and I'd feel tired all day.

I started going into a decline with it all. I just felt permanently sick. I had to force myself to eat. When I went to bed at night I'd only sleep a few hours, and then I'd have a dream and I'd be wide-awake. The dreams were always really frightening, about Jacqui and the baby. It got so I hated to sleep at all, yet at the same time I just wished I could fall asleep and sleep for a month or even never wake up again at all.

I started going into cemeteries and looking at tombstones. I'd be driving along when I'd see a cemetery coming up ahead, and without really knowing it I'd turn in at the gate and spend an hour wandering among the tombstones. It was the only thing made me feel peaceful. One day they'd carry me into a place like that and I'd stop feeling miserable. It seems funny, but that cheered me up. When something's really hurting you'd do anything to make it stop, even die. Death doesn't seem any problem when your life's really miserable, you get a feeling of real happiness when you think of it. All the tombstones were marked "AT PEACE" or "AT REST." I'd never thought of that before, but I could really see the meaning of it all now.

I remember hoping I'd die soon, because another thing I was scared of was going insane. Sometimes I wasn't quite sure if I was all there. I started behaving like a lunatic myself.

For instance, one night I had a runner. (That's someone who takes a taxi ride, then tries to get away without paying.) Usually I don't take too much notice. It's one of the aggravations of the job, you get one every hundred or so trips. I usually let them go if it's going to be too much trouble. What the fare usually says is, "I'll just get the money in the house." Then he disappears inside for ten minutes and leaves you waiting in the road. He's hoping you'll get fed up and go away without being paid. He's watching you all the time from behind the curtains.

They're usually the sort of two-bit little crooks who try and fiddle everything, pinching glasses out of pubs and spoons out of cafés. When you ring the bell they don't answer. You normally just mark them down, so they can't come near the firm again. They spend half their lives dodging people they owe money to. They get on a sort of blacklist the firm keeps. They can't get a taxi till they pay what's owing, and once they've done it once, they never get a lift without paying first at the office.

This time I rang the bell and hit the knocker a couple of times, but he pretended he hadn't heard it. Normally I'd have gone away and forgotten about it, but this particular night a sort of rage got hold of me and before I knew what I'd done, I'd kicked the door in.

I don't know who was more surprised, me or the fare. He came dashing up the hall, yelling about damages and calling the police. (He was one of those little pimp types. He reminded me of Jacqui's dad, in fact.)

I just called his bluff.

"That's a good idea," I said. "You call the law and I'll get them to make you pay your fare."

"You miserable bastard," he said, "making all this fuss over a lousy couple of quid."

He called me a load of filth all the way back to my car, and even threw a brick or something at me as I drove off, but luckily he missed.

But I was horrified at myself afterward. What a stupid way for me to behave! You wouldn't last a week in taxiing if you carried on like that all the time.

Another time, I had this terrible nightmare. It was the most frightening thing that ever happened to me in my whole life. I dreamt I was walking down a dark street and I met Jacqui. She was standing under a lamp post, like a pro, and she gave me the eye, and I took her home to bed.

Then during the night I woke up and it was pitch-black and I couldn't see a thing, only hear Jacqui breathing alongside of me in the bed. There seemed to be something wrong with her, something different. I tried to see her face, but it was so dark I couldn't make anything out at all. So I started to feel her all over, and somehow she was a different shape. She was all hard and hairy, all over, and her legs went very thin at the bottom. She frightened the life out of me. I was so frightened, I felt like screaming. What I was realizing, in this dream, was that she'd turned into a goat. Not an ordinary friendly goat, but like you see the Devil sometimes, with his cloven hoofs. It frightened the bloody life out of me. I woke up in the middle of the night and turned all the lights on, I was that scared. I was whimpering like a little kid. I felt I'd have given anything to have some woman there, some kind woman I could have just crept up against and had her cuddle me and make me feel safe again.

Around that time I clicked with another girl, a really nice one, a nurse. I took a little kid to hospital, who'd had a bang in an accident, and I got talking to the nurse in casualty, and we really liked one another.

She was a really beautiful girl, Janie, clean, intelligent, good looking. Any other time we'd have got a thing going inside a couple of weeks, but with Jacqui around, nothing happened at all. I just couldn't let it. I really fancied Janie, and I think she fancied me. She called around to the house a couple of times to see me. But nothing happened. I just felt you couldn't have one girl expecting your baby, then go off with another, no matter what the girl expecting your baby was up to. I *knew* Jacqui was bad for me. I *knew* she was lying, cheating, wasting my money. But she was still having my little boy, and I couldn't just ditch her.

You get this feeling you've just got to sacrifice yourself for your children. You can't help yourself. You're like one of these seeds that hangs on a tree all fat and sassy, and you drop to the ground, and then you either make a shoot or go black and rotten. You see that with chestnuts on the trees in the garden. When they're on the tree they're in these big, strong cases with spikes all over them. They're so strong you've got to break them by putting them under your shoe. And inside there's a beautiful tight, shiny chestnut. But when that drops to the ground it shrivels right up and goes rotten and wrinkled.

It's just like that with people. When you're in your teens you look around you at all these shriveled up old people, and you wonder how the hell they ever got that way. You can see it's working too much and looking after kids and you say to yourself, "That's not going to happen to me, boy. When I'm older and earning good money, I'm going to spend it on something sensible, like sports cars and holidays by the Med. I'm not going to be working eight days a week to bring up a bunch of kids who hardly even know I'm a person."

And then you reach a certain age and it suddenly hits you. All you can think of to do is have kids and spend all your time and money bringing them up so they can leave you. You have to be mad. It seems the best idea in the world to get some girl pregnant and have her pushing out this little wet embryo. At the time you're in your prime, you're fat and sleek like the chestnuts on the tree. And you can no more hang on to the tree than they can. You know when you fall you're going to lose your own life trying to make another, but it still doesn't worry you. You think, "I'll get old and die, but my kids will go on living in my place." You're kidding yourself, of course. Kids don't go on living in *your* place, they're living in their *own* place.

I couldn't seem to do anything to help myself. I'd think, "I won't phone Jacqui, I won't see her again. If I can just get away from her for a month or two, this feeling will wear off."

Then I'd go to sleep and have these really vivid dreams about the baby. He'd be in his big bubble, and he'd be looking at me and holding out his little hands to me. He'd be all loving, and lost, so I'd feel my heart was breaking abandoning him like that. I'd think, "What sort of a life will he have with just his mother looking after him, a lunatic woman, and all sorts of sick people coming into his home?"

I'd get these really horrific thoughts in my head, about him being a beautiful little boy, and Jacqui's bent friends creeping into his bedroom to molest him. I could even see her little queer father doing it.

I kept doing the maddest things to protect him. I thought, "Whatever I do, I mustn't give Jacqui an excuse for disappearing with him. She'll crucify the poor little child."

I gave her more or less an open line to my money. Every time I saw her I'd give her a fiver or so. You give someone a fiver every time you see them, and they don't mind seeing you a lot. I went through hundreds like that.

I tried to make her eat properly, too, and keep off the drink, to give the baby inside her a chance. I'd buy pounds of fruit and salad at the market and give them to her every time I saw her.

She just wasted my money left, right and center. One time she cost me about fifty pounds in one day. That was when she got me involved in the most sordid bit of taxiing I've ever done in my life. Her grandmother died, and Jacqui wanted to go to Sussex to clean out the old lady's house, and I ended up driving her, and her mother and her sister for miles down all these tiny little lanes. That was a really hellish drive. Normally I wouldn't ever take a complainer in my car, and here I was, stuck with a whole family of them. No one offered to pay for the petrol, of course, and every time I stopped they all wanted drinks, chocolate, fish and chips, all paid for by me. And their conversation was as putrid as their manners. Literally all they could talk about was sex, who was screwing with who, etc. etc. etc.

According to them, just about everyone you ever heard of was bent. They started with Hollywood, went through the Houses of Parliament, and ended up with the Grenadier Guards. There wasn't one normal person in the lot of them—everyone was bending for everyone else. About the only public figure they didn't get around to was the Pope, and I think that was only because he'd just died.

They never mentioned a single other subject the entire twelve hours I was with them.

It was like being with three blind people. We went through some lovely countryside and beautiful little villages, but no one ever commented. None of them even noticed a pretty cottage or a bridge over a little river.

They were the sort of people you could take to Shangri-La and all they'd notice was the yak droppings.

I should have dumped them on the side of the road and scooted.

But I was completely insane at that time. You know what I did? I blamed myself for it all. I kept saying to myself, "What have you done to make Jacqui like this? You must be boring and stupid. If you were a really nice person, she'd be glad to give up dropping her knickers and settle down with a lovely little baby."

I tried to understand Jacqui's point of view. I tried to see the whole thing from the woman's angle. I told myself, women get fed up with marriage and kids. When they're little girls they dream of being ballet dancers or riding horses. Then, when they grow up, they find themselves washing dishes and wiping behinds morning, noon, and night. They get depressed. They don't get much support from the husband. By the time they've got 1.7 kids, or 2.4 kids, or whatever it is, he's so busy doing overtime at work they hardly ever see him. They burn him a round of toast in the morning and incinerate a pan of fish fingers at night, and that's about the lot, except at weekends. All the rest of the time, they're stuck with screaming kids. They can't go anywhere because the kids make a mess of every trip out. It takes about two hours just to get them ready, what with having to put everything on for them, and them taking it all off again as soon as your back's turned. Then you no sooner get halfway to where you're going, than they want the potty. And if you don't make with it fast, you've got to take them straight back to the house smelling of roses.

I thought perhaps Jacqui was seeing that ahead of her. Perhaps she felt she was going to miss out on the glamorous side of life.

I was just being stupid, of course. I didn't mind a bit Jacqui's wanting to be something glamorous, I'd have *paid* for her to have ballet lessons or learn to ride a horse.

But she wasn't interested. What *she* wanted was to be a total lowlife, which would be a million times more sordid than being a mother.

The strain started to affect me. I started to get this really peculiar feeling. I felt as though I was turning gray. Not just my hair, but my whole body. I felt sort of lifeless, as though all my skin was turning to rubbish. I felt like a man who'd been living in a cellar for years. Not a basement flat with furniture and carpets and heating, but just a bare, empty cellar, all damp and dark, full of cobwebs. You know when you put something down a cellar that's like that—a bike or a washing machine—in no time it's all mildewed and rusted and it hardly works.

That's the way I felt, in my whole body and mind.

I went everywhere in slow motion. When I was cabbying before, I used to jump out of the taxi and open the doors for people and carry their bags. But now I just sort of slumped behind the wheel all the time.

I was neglecting the house, too. I couldn't take an interest in it. When you came into the hall and the sun was shining, you could see a layer of dust where the floors weren't polished and on the hall table and right up the stairs and bannister rail to the next floor.

People at work started commenting on the way I looked. They started telling me I should see a doctor. I did. He gave me a check over. He was wasting his time. There was no way I was going to tell him what was really the matter with me. I felt sorry for him and all the other doctors. People came to doctors sick because their lives are all cocked up, but they keep quiet about it, and the poor bloke's always working in the dark. He wastes his time checking them over and wastes the pharmacist's time prescribing bottles of tonic and colored pills.

I tried to cheer myself up with that trick of imagining all those people suffering with the same problem. But it just made me more depressed. It was like being a leper and thinking of the millions of others whose noses and toes were dropping off, too.

I couldn't even cheer myself up by thinking I was a special, interesting case. There were lots of blokes in the same boat. There were even worse cases than mine. There was this lord had his name in the paper just then because his wife was banging around like an unlatched door on a windy night. At least my business was private, while his was splashed all over the papers for everyone to gloat over. There wasn't anything special about me, I was just a typical product of a clash between a man and a woman.

There was even a poor old blackbird getting the same sort of thing out in the garden just then. Him and his mate were nesting in a pile of thorn branches I'd trimmed by the back fence. Did she treat *him* like dirt! *She* chose the place, *she* decided how the nest was going to be built, *she* was the gaffer while he did the laboring. The poor old cock was slaving all day bringing the mud and sticks. And if he brought mud or sticks *she* didn't like, she bashed him around the face and pecked at him.

And it wasn't just the big things that were horrible, the

little things were disgusting too, the sort of tiny little details you'd hardly even notice.

Take one time I was just going shopping with Jacqui, and she and this little pouf started making eyes at one another. That's what you're up against. You've got a woman walking alongside you who's supposed to be yours—you're feeding her, looking after her, she's carrying your child inside her—and she starts making eyes at some creep, right in the main road.

You'd think there would be some sort of sacred bond between the two of you, something you could trust. You'd think if there was anything in the whole world could bring two people together, it would be having a child together. Only a few hours before, you were lying in each other's arms, touching each other all over, telling how you loved one another. You felt really close, welded together, as though you'd become one person instead of two. You were planning your whole future together, you were going to spend a lifetime with one another, bringing up your children.

And then all of a sudden one squalid little guy comes down the road and gives your woman the eye, and the whole thing blows up in your face.

I wouldn't have minded so much if he'd been a decent-looking lad, but he was just a pimp. He was one of those really petty little blokes who's always combing his hair or shrinking his jeans. They usually work somewhere they don't have to get their hands dirty, at some girl's job. But Jacqui's eyes lit up when she saw him. You could see she was wishing I wasn't there, so she could go off and screw with this guy. The thought flashed across my mind then, "There's nothing you'll ever do with this woman, mate. You could take her to a desert island and she'd still find some little pimp to bang with."

I realized then that love between the sexes is a cutthroat business. There's no real loyalty between a man and a woman. It's true when they say a standing prick has no conscience. Once a man or woman gets horny, they don't have any principles. A wife will cheat on her husband, or a husband on his wife, and think nothing of it, if they've found someone who turns them on.

Everyone knows it. Everyone goes through it. It's just one of the hazards you accept in life, like toothache, or piles, or getting run over.

Chapter

T hen there was the last day of her life. For some reason I seem to remember every tiny detail about that, every word she said, everything I did and felt.

Jacqui wasn't living at my place then. She'd insisted on going to stay at her mother's, with the randy little drunk, and all the prostitution going on, and with my baby inside her. She said her mother needed her, whatever that meant. What her mother *needed* was a three-year course in human decency.

I was worried to death. I felt as though I'd hardly slept or eaten for weeks. I'd telephoned her every day, and she finally agreed to come down to my place.

I was hoping for so much from that visit. For one thing, it was a really beautiful day, one of those April days that's just like summer. We'd had a lot of early warm weather that year, and the daffodils were out in the garden, the leaves were coming out on the trees, the birds were building their nests. I was really looking forward to Jacqui's coming. I was like a kid looking forward to the circus. I cleaned the house from top to bottom, thawed out a chicken from the freezer, put a bottle of red wine to warm to room temperature, got a load of salad things and fruit.

For some reason I thought we might get a fresh start, the day being so bright and the winter being nearly over and all. You know how it is in the movies. The sun comes out, the birds are singing, and everything starts going right again. I thought it might all get through to Jacqui some-how, purify her mind. I'd forgotten she'd already seen eighteen springs and summers. I'd forgotten the little worm and the cowpat. Jacqui's idea of the best way to spend the first day of spring would probably be to go for a nice stroll down Park Lane at midnight.

But a man stuck with a stupid woman's got to keep hoping she'll change, otherwise he'll go mad.

She said she'd come at twelve. I wasn't really expecting her to be on time, she never was, but when it got to one o'clock I phoned her mother's to see what time she'd left. Of course, she was still there, at her mother's. I'd been waiting all morning, and she hadn't even moved out of the house. She'd only just got out of bed, in fact. I could feel my heart start to race, really pounding in my ears.

When she finally got to the phone, I tried to sound casual, but I was feeling so sick. I knew everything she was going to say before she opened her mouth, I'd had the same sort of stupidity so many times already. Still, I asked her if something had happened.

"Oh no," she said, "I just got up late." She could have got up early and had a whole morning in the sun. I could imagine her at the other end of the wire, in that stinking flat, with all the windows shut and the curtains drawn, and the drunken flies crawling all over the furniture. I wondered why I was bothering. I said I'd been waiting for her.

"Have you? What on earth for?"

She always did that when she'd done something grotty, pretended I was making a fuss out of nothing. I reminded her she'd said she'd be down at twelve.

"Did I? Oh well, I forgot. I mean, I didn't realize you'd be expecting me or anything."

She knew that was a lie. In all the time I'd known her, I'd always had everything ready whenever she'd come down.

I asked her what time she'd be arriving then.

"Oh, I can't possibly come down yet. I've only just got up. My sister's in the bathroom. I have to wash, put on my makeup. I won't be leaving for another hour."

I felt exhausted to death with months of trying to get through to her.

"You can come as you are," I said, "you can have your bath here."

"But my makeup!"

The stupid bloody makeup, always these stupid women and their stupid bloody makeup. They have a life, a chance to breathe and see and meet people, and they throw it all away to sit down in front of a dusty mirror painting their faces.

"Can't you come without it?" I was trying to be calm, but I was all sort of shaking inside.

"Don't be stupid. I look terrible without my makeup."

"But I don't mind. I prefer you without it." I thought my opinion might mean something. Some hope! She thought more of what strangers on the road thought than anything *I* might feel.

"You don't know what you're asking," she said, "I can't go out without my makeup."

I had to give her ten more points for bloody-minded stupidity. She was going to wreck the whole day, and there was nothing I could do about it.

"Well, when you've done that, how long will you be?"

"Then I have to go to the bank and get some money. Oh, and my mother's shopping and things. Are you there?"

"Yes," I said, and I just couldn't help sounding weary, I was that fed up.

Jacqui was on to it straight away. That was another of her tricks. She'd keep on being stupid till you showed you were fed up, then she'd pounce on you for being moody and difficult. "What's the matter now?" she said. I told her nothing was the matter.

"Yes there is. What is it?" She was like a headmistress. "Come on, tell me."

I thought how impossible it was to explain to her. If a woman's so bloody insensitive she can't see these things for herself, how in a million years can you get her to understand?

I finally said it was a beautiful day, and if she was late we'd miss it.

"Oh, is that all?"

What a shabby mind she had! She could throw away a whole beautiful day in spring and say, "Is that all?"

I wanted to say to her then, "Look, don't bother. Paint your face, wash yourself, take a running jump at yourself. Don't come to see me, I don't want your charity." But I couldn't say it. I *did* want her charity. I'd had a couple of happy hours because I'd thought she was coming. Now I was back to square one at the thought she might not be coming at all. Her stupidity was driving me mad. I fell back on the only thing I could.

"How's the baby?" I said.

"Oh, he's fine."

"And his mother?"

"She's fine, too."

"No pains or sickness today?"

"None at all, thank you."

"Well, don't rush. Just come down when you can."

"All right. 'Bye." If phones had elbows I'd have got one in the ribs. She couldn't get rid of me fast enough.

"Goodbye," I said, but she'd gone already.

I needed about three tries to get the receiver back on the rest, my hands were shaking so much. My heart was racing worse too, so bad I couldn't seem to breathe. I'd have to find something to pass the time. I was much too churned up to read or think, so I went through the house checking to see if everything was tidy. I switched on all the fires, as well as the central heating, in case Jacqui started complaining about the cold.

The sunlight was coming through the windows and the bedspread didn't look perfectly fresh and clean. I changed it for another one. I thought of running out and buying her a bunch of flowers, as a surprise. But I couldn't leave the house. She might phone to say she wanted picking up someplace and bringing here.

I felt really jumpy, looking every few minutes at the time. I decided to clean the car. Maybe the fresh air would make me feel better. I did it slowly, to be still doing it when Jacqui arrived. She'd see me busy, know I hadn't been fretting waiting for her. The inside of the car was full of empty drink cans and fish-and-chips wrappers her mother and sister had stuffed down behind the seats. I vacuumed the carpets, cleaned under them, polished the dash, cleaned the inside of the windows, washed the body-work and waxed it.

It was nearly dark by the time Jacqui turned up, so I had to have the light on in the garage. I was checking the pressure in the spare tire when I heard her footsteps behind me on the gravel.

I tried my best to look casual before I turned around, but I realized I was wasting my time when I saw her. Her face was really brutal, as though she was determined to pick a fight with me. She was wearing her tart's outfit: her shortie pullover, her sheepskin jacket, and her skintight jeans. God knows how she was cramming a five-month pregnancy into that lot, the poor baby must have been stifled. When I laid her out in her tomb I bought beautiful things for her, a long black silk skirt and a beautiful honey-colored silk blouse. Those are the clothes she wears now. The jeans and other things I cleaned and kept with her. Not because I liked them, but because they were hers and she might not have wanted me to throw them away.

"Hello," I said to her. I was telling myself, whatever else, I mustn't get annoyed by anything she did. "Did you have an easy journey?"

"I felt sick." She said it as though it was *my* fault, of course. I'll bet she'd been eating all kinds of supermarket rubbish at her mother's, and getting through at least one bottle of wine a day. I tried to give her a little kiss of welcome. She did the stiff-shoulder routine and sucked her lips in against her teeth. I pretended I hadn't noticed. I told her to go in the house while I finished off the car.

She stuck out her hand and said, "Where's the key?" I'd given her the key to the front door in case she ever wanted to come down while I was out. I asked her where it was.

"I've lost it, give me yours." I gave her my key. I'd have to change the lock now, in case one of her family or friends burgled me. When I gave her the key, I noticed her wedding ring was missing.

"Where's your ring?" I asked her.

"Oh, I sold it. I was hard up, so I went to one of those little shops that buys scrap gold, and I sold it."

My hands were starting to shake again. I was wondering if I could get through the rest of the evening. I couldn't even decide whether to finish the car quickly or take another ten minutes over it. If I rushed it, she might say I never left her alone. If I was slow, she'd say I was sulking. I timed myself exactly five minutes more then went inside.

Jacqui was in the kitchen, looking in the fridge. As I came in she took the orange juice out, unscrewed the cap, and poured some down her throat. She didn't sip it or drink it, she just poured it down this big throat she had. Next, she took the lid off a container of cottage cheese. It was half-full. She found the ketchup and dolloped in as much ketchup as there was cheese, mixed it all up with a teaspoon and started eating it. I wanted to get out of the kitchen before she made me sick, but stayed and started getting the chicken ready. I was thinking, "Maybe she's nasty because she's ravenous." She must have been living on the smell from the lavatory in that flat of her mother's. If I gave her a really nice meal she might change, she might realize she was much better off with me and stay and have the baby properly.

But she'd made up her mind to be nasty. While I was getting the chicken ready, I made her a cup of tea and put it in front of her. She did the same trick as with the book on pregnancy.

"Did I ask for this?" she said.

"No, I just thought you'd like it."

"Well I don't." She marched across the kitchen and dumped it down the sink.

Then, when she'd finished being a pig in my kitchen, she decided she'd like to wash her hair and be a pig in my bathroom for a change. She'd wasted half the day lying in bed, and now she wanted to waste the other half washing her hair.

When I followed her into the bathroom, she was shivering and wrapping her arms around herself and whining about the cold. She really was trying to be difficult. It was seventy degrees Fahrenheit on the room thermometer. There were two radiators going full blast, and I even had the ceiling heater on.

I said I'd turn up the heating. I was determined she wasn't going to annoy me. I put the boiler thermostat up to a hundred-and-seventy degrees Fahrenheit. Nearly boiling. It wouldn't have any effect for nearly an hour, but when I got back to the bathroom Jacqui had decided it was warmer there already. She'd stopped shivering and was moping about twiddling at the taps.

"How am I going to wash my hair here?" she said. "What am I going to do?"

The bathroom had a bath, with a built-in shower arrangement, and a washbasin, with one of those push-on hair sprays. I suggested to Jacqui she could either stand at the basin and wash her hair or fill up the bathtub and wash it as she sat in there.

She looked all around the bathroom as though it was an outside lav or something.

"Haven't you anything better?" You'd have thought she was used to solid gold taps and Nubian slaves. When you think of the bathroom she'd been used to at her mother's place, with all the crud and stinks! I wouldn't have rinsed off my gardening boots in *their* tub. But you often get that with people, the ones with the lousiest home life put on the biggest airs.

"This is a house," I said, "not a hairdresser's." I meant her to see what a ratbag she was being, but she just said "What a pity," in a way that put my beautiful house lower than every pimpy little High Street hair parlor she'd ever been in.

She finally decided the best way to do her hair would be to kneel by the bath and hang her head over. I couldn't have thought of anything more awkward if you'd given me a week. I could see she was going to have a real struggle, so I said I'd help her. She brightened up right away.

"Oh, will you?" she said, "How nice. I *hate* washing my hair. All sorts of people offer to help me with it, but none of them can stand it to the end. They always leave me to finish it off myself."

It's stupid isn't it, but I found myself feeling sorry for Jacqui again, she couldn't even find anyone to help her with her hair. She was so rude and vicious with me, but one kind word and I was at her feet again.

"I'll help you," I said, "right to the end."

"Promise?" she said. "Oh, but you'll give up. You'll see, you won't carry on till the finish."

"I will, though. If I break an arm and a leg, I'll still carry on till it's completely done."

I finally managed to get her started. She took about five minutes to get herself settled where she wanted, all the time squealing, "I'm freezing!" and "Oh, how awful!" and "Ow, my knees are killing me!" she had to undo the front of her jeans before she could kneel down at all. Then she unpinned her hair and hung her head over the edge of the bath.

I asked her if she wasn't going to take her pullover off.

"What for? I never take it off in the hairdresser's, do I? What do you want me to take it off now for?"

What a bloody stupid question! I wanted her to take it off because I wanted to *see* her. I wanted to see the woman who was having my baby, I wanted to see the way her stomach was going around and her nipples were changing, like it said in the book.

If she'd been a proper woman she'd want to show me all that, want me to be pleased with her, proud of her.

But how could you explain that to a woman like Jacqui? She was about as sensitive as the china slab in a public urinal. How can you explain things like that to a woman who can't see them on her own?

We finally started on the hair washing. Jacqui knelt at the bath, and I stood with the shower attachment, wetting her hair. As soon as the water touched her head, she squealed, "Oh, it's too hot, it's too hot!" I'd spent about a minute trying it out on the back of my hand to get it exactly right.

"Make it cooler!"

I turned the regulator one degree toward the cool side. As soon as she felt the change Jacqui yelled, "Brrr! It's too cold, make it warmer!"

I turned the regulator back to where I'd had it before.

"Ah," she said, "that's better. Why didn't you have it like that at the beginning, instead of burning me?"

None of that deserved an answer, so I just carried on with her hair. They say your hair keeps on growing after you're dead. Jacqui's didn't, I remember noticing. Even months afterward her hair seemed to be about the same length, and her nails. Growing hair was one thing Jacqui was good at. It sprouted on her head thicker than anyone I'd ever seen before, and it came out over her whole body. If she'd had as much brains and decency as she had hair I'd never have had the problems with her I did have.

We went through the whole ritual: shampooing, rinsing, squeezing dry, conditioning, rinsing, squeezing dry. Of course, I had the wrong shampoo, and the wrong conditioner, and it was going to make her hair an awful mess, etc. etc. And the water was always too hot or too cold, or there wasn't enough of it, or too much, or I was rubbing too hard, or not hard enough, or I was interfering and spoiling it, or when on earth was I going to give her a hand like I'd promised.

Then, when I wrapped her hair up, the towel was too thick, and the next one I used was too small, so she dragged all my towels out of the linen cupboard till she found one she liked, then wrapped her head in it while I folded up the others and put them all away again.

Then, while her hair was drying, she decided she was hungry. I tried to organize a civilized meal. I set the table in the kitchen, put out wineglasses and salad and napkins, but she just did her trick of wolfing the whole chicken herself. She didn't even put it on her plate. She just picked it to pieces in the baking tray and threw the bones back in as she finished with them. She left those, and the skin, for me.

Then, when she'd eaten the whole chicken and her hair was dry, she suddenly jumped up and said, "Well, I have to get back to town now. Bye-bye."

You'd have thought I'd be glad to hear her say that, you'd think I'd be glad to see the back of her. If anyone in the world but your woman or your kids behaved the way she did, you'd kick them out of the house. Only family could be so disgusting and get away with it.

But I wasn't glad. When she said she was going, I felt as terrible as though the world was coming to an end.

What I should have done was said "Right!" and kicked her out in the street and forgotten about her. But I couldn't. I'd been looking forward to her staying the night so much it was nearly killing me. It wasn't sex, I just wanted to be near my baby and the woman who was having him.

She'd have gone off then, only when she got as far as the hall, something turned her on. Probably it was the sight of me being dead miserable. Maybe she had a sadistic streak. Some doctors think *all* women are sadomasochistic. They're either kicking their men around, or letting their kids kick *them* around. It gives them the hots. I read a book about the First World War once, and this guy reckoned the women used to get sexy thinking of all the thousands of soldiers being machine-gunned on the Western Front. He was there at the time, so he should know. And anyway, if you've had any experience with women, you could believe it.

That was the only relief with Jacqui, when she went sexy. She'd become all soft and tender and even intelligent. When she wasn't being sexy she was like a big brutal animal.

But I was thankful for small mercies. I crept into bed with her. My body seemed to be aching all over, in all its joints. I felt really worn-out and so weak that even getting up on my elbows was a terrible effort. I did a really nice job for her. I was very careful not to put any weight on the baby and then got her talking about what she'd been doing since I saw her last. She started going on about her mother and sister, all sorts of tittle-tattle. She hadn't read any good books or thought any good thoughts in those weeks. She'd probably spent half the time fiddling with her eyebrows and her nails and the other half talking about who was banging who in the neighborhood.

But I was happy just to let her chatter on while I cuddled her. I was really high on the baby. Jacqui's stomach had started to come out all hard and round, and it tickled me absolutely pink just to lie beside her and stroke it, and put my head on it and see if I could hear the baby or feel him kicking.

All I could hear, of course, was Jacqui's juices battling to digest a four-pound chicken, but I was still happy with myself. I thought of all that food going to make the baby beautiful, to shape his little fingers and toes. It was really a fantastic thing to have this woman making a baby for you inside herself, creating another human being, someone you'd really love and get tremendous happiness from. I got all my old feelings back, about piggybacking him up to bed nights, and him all laughing. About sitting by his bedside and watching his little face while he slept, and tucking him in. About him splashing around in his swimming pool and seeing his little arms and legs going brown and silky in the sun. I got tears in my eyes thinking about it, and I felt all choked, I loved him so much. I felt I'd do anything for Jacqui, that she was having him for me.

Chapter

5

Lying there like that, I started to think my luck had changed. People always do that. You can be living an absolute dog's life for ages, for years, then after five minutes of good luck or kindness you think your luck's changed forever.

It hasn't, of course, you're just getting a breather.

It's like when you were a kid and you were tormenting an ant's nest. You'd wreck their nest, then watch them try to patch it up, without poking your stick in anymore. The ants probably think the same thing as you do, that things are getting better, and it's just when they're thinking that, and thanking the great god of the ants, that your kettle full of water on the gas stove gets just nicely boiled.

I was like the ants. I was lying next to Jacqui, patching my little wrecked life together, when Jacqui started.

She kicked off by telling me about this brothelly club she'd gone to one night where girls go as "hostesses" and get the customers to buy them drinks. She'd spent half the night talking to some Dutchman, and at the end he'd given her five pounds for her trouble and gone back to his own hotel. Then Jacqui had left the club at three in the morning to go home herself.

She went quiet then. I was lying with my head on her stomach, waiting for her to start again, but she didn't, so I sat up in bed with this horrible crawling sensation going all over me.

"What happened then?" I said, wondering why I was even bothering to ask. I *knew* what she was going to say.

Then she told me the rest. On her way home she'd let herself be picked up by a curb crawler. He'd offered her a lift in his Jaguar, taken her back to his flat, fed her drink, and screwed her. Just like that, and her five months pregnant.

There are times in your life when you think you're miserable, when you think you're about as unhappy as you can get, that you've really hit rock bottom. And then suddenly something else happens so much worse that you realize you weren't down before, you were really happy compared with what you are now. If you could get from here to when you thought you were miserable, you'd be the happiest man alive. I was like that when Jacqui told me about the curb crawler. I'd been thinking I was really low just before that, and I suddenly discovered I could go down about another million miles before I touched bottom.

I didn't know what to say. I didn't know what to do. I felt like one of those computers when it's asked to answer the impossible question, and it just gets hotter and hotter till it melts all its wires.

My mind just kept zapping around like the ball in a pinball machine. Different thoughts kept lighting up: the baby, Jacqui, me. Me, Jacqui, the baby.

I had this really horrific picture of the baby inside Jacqui, and the two of them mauled and squashed by this creepy little curb crawler.

A curb crawler! Everyone knows how bent they are. They're always being arrested for indecent assault, or they're murdering someone. And Jacqui lets herself be picked up by one, gets in his car, even goes back to his place with him.

I'd been lying in bed feeling warm and lovely for the first time in weeks, and now I felt as lonely and cold as if I'd been dumped stark naked in some field in Siberia.

The thought kept banging around in my head, "Why does she do these things?" She had a lovely home to come to, I was keeping her, I'd always looked after her well, never hit her or insulted her.

It wasn't even as if I was ugly or anything. The guys she was going with were all sorts of creeps and perverts. I was Clark Gable compared with most of them. I could hardly talk, I was sort of choking.

"Christ," I said at last, "what did you want to go doing that for?" I felt absolutely numb from head to foot. I felt I was shriveling up to nothing, and yet at the same time I wanted to vomit. "What did you go doing that for?" I said again.

She just sort of shrugged and looked blank. I really think she must have been lunatic.

"I was fed up," she said at last. "I was at that rotten club half the night and all I made was five pounds. I was walking home fed up and I just did it."

It was really useless ever asking Jacqui a question. All you ever got from her was a stupid answer like that one, that was about a hundred times worse than no answer at all.

"But Jesus, woman, I was *here.* All you had to do was pick up a phone and I'd have come and got you."

I don't think I'd ever seen the night looking so black in my life before. Jacqui had put me through the hoop a dozen times in the last few months, but this one was definitely the worst. I had a feeling like something was coming out of the blackness and crushing me flat.

I was going mad, I think.

"Don't you realize what you're doing?" I said. "That child's inside you. Your body is the only home he's got. And you go filthying up his home and putting him in danger by screwing with all these dirty old men you pick up. What on earth is that kid going to think of you when it grows up?"

She just looked at me with her blank look and said, "It won't think anything. How's it going to know?"

128

"Because I'm going to bloody well tell it, that's how!" I said. "When that kid's old enough I'm going to tell it what you did to it."

You'd have thought *that* would have got through to her. You'd have thought she'd have realized then how bloody grotesquely she was carrying on. But all she did was look at me with real hatred in her face and say, "I do believe you're the sort of swine who'd play a mean trick like that."

You couldn't get through to her, you just really couldn't get through.

I couldn't think what to do. What I did was get one of the maddest ideas of my whole life. You won't believe what a crazy notion I got, but it will just show you how my mind was working. I thought what I should do was get in touch with this curb crawler guy and tell him to lay off Jacqui.

I'd have gone out in the middle of the night, to where Jacqui said he'd taken her, but she said I needn't bother, she had his phone number in her handbag. She also said if I did phone him ("bother him at all," was how she put it), she'd never see me again. But I dug his number out of her bag and went ahead anyway.

I've had to do some really awful things in my time, but making that phone call was one of the worst. My hands were shaking so much I could hardly dial. I thought at first he wasn't going to answer. It was about two in the morning, maybe he was out doing his curb-crawling bit, or perhaps he'd picked himself up another willing whore, but finally he came on the line. I didn't like him from the first. I'd been hoping he might be a decent sort of bloke, one you could talk to, even in the circumstances. But even the way he said "Hello" made me think of one of those little curs that's always yapping on people's doorsteps.

In normal life he was the sort of guy I wouldn't even have bothered talking to, he was such a little mongrel. But I had to discuss my woman and child with him and beg him to leave them alone.

"Look," I said, "I'm phoning about Jacqui, the girl you picked up the other night." Straight away he snapped back, "Are you her father?"

"No," I said. My voice probably sounded really peculiar. "I'm the father of the baby she's expecting. She's five-months pregnant. She shouldn't have done what she did the other night, and I'm asking you not to see her again. I want to keep her here till the baby's born."

I know! It sounds incredibly stupid now, but that's what I said to him. I didn't swear or shout, I was just very polite and reasonable. If *he*'d been any good he'd have been polite back, but my first guess about him was right, he was just a mongrel.

"I don't want to discuss this with you," he said. "Anything Jacqui has to tell me, she'll tell me herself. Is she there? Let me speak to her."

I held the phone out but Jacqui just shook her head and looked murder at me. I held the handset right up to her mouth but she just sucked her lips in and wouldn't talk.

"She's here with me in bed," I said to the guy, "but she doesn't want to speak to you."

I realized afterward how rough that must have been on

him, being phoned at two in the morning and told his bird was in bed with another bloke. I mean, he probably thought she was *his* bird, the same way I thought she was mine.

But I still think he was a cur. Instead of believing me, he called me a liar. He sort of sneered at me before he banged the phone down, "I don't believe any of this. I think you're just a bloody little liar. I shall be seeing Jacqui tomorrow, and I know she'll tell me you've made all this up."

She would, too. I'll bet Jacqui could have talked him around with no trouble. He a curb crawler, she a pro, and they'd get their heads together and brand me as a rat for trying to be decent toward my kid.

When I put the phone down, Jacqui said, "That's it. It's all off between us. I won't have you interfering in my private life and humiliating me. I'm not going to see you any more. The chap you've just spoken to has offered to set me up in a flat. I was only thinking about it before, but now I'm definitely going to take it."

So that was the picture. Jacqui would be seeing this guy again tomorrow, and he'd be screwing her with my little baby inside her. She'd never come to see me again, or let me see the child, and the poor little bugger would be brought up with a mad mother and the likes of drunks, prostitutes, and curb crawlers for family and friends. If it was a little girl it would probably be doing it for money at thirteen. If it was a boy it would probably be perverted and queening it at the same age.

I realize now that what I should have done, when

Jacqui threatened to go off with the curb crawler, was beat her. I should have punched her head into the pillow. I should have broken her nose and knocked her teeth out so no one would want her. Her little curb crawler wouldn't waste his money on a flat for a woman with a broken nose and false teeth. I might have got six months in prison for grievous bodily harm, but it would have been worth it to have the baby safe.

But I didn't.

I didn't do a thing.

I think that's one of the big problems, why women go so wild these days. Men are too civilized, they don't attack them. A man being had by his woman *should* go berserk and beat her till she can't move. But he doesn't, he's too inhibited. *She* behaves like a raving lunatic, and *he* holds himself in check and tries to be reasonable. So the woman gets no guidance. She depends on the man to tell her how to behave.

A woman despises a man who's soft with her when she's unfaithful. She expects to get a hiding, and she's happier when she does. That's what any sensible bloke did years ago, he'd just push her up against a wall with one hand and punch some sense into her with the other.

I should have done that to Jacqui, beaten her up. I had her there, in the house. No one would have heard her yelling, and if she'd called the police afterward I could either have told them the circumstances or said she was lying and someone else had done it. It would have served her right, being treated like that, after the way she'd behaved toward me and the baby.

But instead of doing something sensible like beating Jacqui up, I found myself in the bathroom trying to kill myself.

I think what happened was, under the strain, my mind went. I didn't seem able to see anything. I felt almost as if I had a big helmet on, and I could only see out of this narrow little slit in the front of it. I took a carload of Americans to one of those jousting contests once, and while I was hanging around, one of the "knights" let me try on his helmet. He was a welder in real life, and he'd made this helmet out of sheet steel. He'd copied it from the real thing in a museum. When you put it on, it sort of squeezed your head all around, and all you could see of the world was a little strip of light, so you had to keep turning your head even to walk around.

That's how I felt that night. I could hardly seem to see enough to make my way to the bathroom. I don't know why I was going to commit suicide, it just seemed a normal enough thing to do in the circumstances. The night felt so black and horrible I didn't want to face any more of it. I had the feeling it was never going to end, that the sun would never come up again, the darkness would go on forever and ever with me having the feeling of being crushed flat and only being able to see things in a little slot. And I just felt I couldn't bear to face it, so I went in the bathroom to kill myself.

You do things like that when you're desperate.

I knew a woman, once, who told me she tried to cut off her head with an axe when she was really low. Her husband gave her a dog's life, and one day she tried to end it all by cutting her head off with an axe. She didn't know what made her choose that way, there must have been thousands of easier ways she could have done it, with a knife, or the gas or anything, but she found herself kneeling down in the kitchen sawing herself on the neck with the axe. Of course, she didn't do any damage. For one thing the axe was blunt (axes in houses are always blunt), and she couldn't get a good swing at herself, as you can imagine. But it does show the sort of lunatic thing you can want to do to yourself.

In my case, I found myself in the bathroom looking for something to cut my wrists with. Afterward I thought how bloody stupid that was. It was Jacqui who had done the dirty trick, not me, yet I wasn't going to hurt her, but myself. I think most suicides must be like that. The tormenter goes scot-free while the poor victim dies a horrible death. I'll bet in most suicides it's the marriage partner drives the other one into doing himself in.

I went all over the bathroom looking for something, but all I could find were cartridge razors, the sort you can only just about nick yourself with. I gave up using the big razor blades years before. The kitchen was just down the hall, with all sorts of sharp knives. But it never occurred to me to go there. People would say, "If you really meant to kill yourself, you'd have gone to the kitchen." That's not true. I really did want to kill myself, but somehow I couldn't think any further than the bathroom, and I didn't think of anything else but razor blades and wrists. I could have gassed myself or gone to the top of the house and thrown myself out of the attic window, but it just never occurred to me.

The woman with the axe told me the same thing happened to *her*. She spent about half an hour trying to position herself for a good swing with the axe. She really wanted to die, but it never occurred to her to try some other way. She didn't even think of sharpening the axe.

It was the same with me. When I couldn't find anything to cut my wrists with, I wandered back into the bedroom and sat on the bed beside Jacqui. I'd got another idea in my mind by then, just as stupid as the idea of killing myself. I felt what I had to do was kill Jacqui instead. I can't imagine what good I thought that was going to do. I think I was more or less out of my mind that whole night.

Jacqui was still lying in bed staring at the ceiling. She could stare at the ceiling more than anyone else I ever met. I think she had so little intelligence, her mind used to go blank for hours at a time. I mean, there'd be nothing at all going on in it, no memories, no thoughts, nothing. She could just switch off and not think anything at all. She didn't even seem to notice me till I sat on the bed and started strangling her.

It would have been much better, of course, if I'd just done something sensible, like breaking both her legs. Seriously, that would have been the right thing to do. If I'd jumped on her knee joints she'd have been unable to walk for at least a year and the baby would have been born safely in hospital. That would have taken a load off my mind and I wouldn't have had to do what I did.

I really must have been out of my mind.

The funny thing was, she didn't try and stop me. She sort of slid along the bed toward me and as good as put her neck in my hands. I said to her, "It's no use. We can't go on like this. You'll make that child terribly unhappy the way you're carrying on. He'd be better off dead."

It was only then she started crying and saying, "Please don't kill me. I don't want to die. I'll do anything. I'll change. I'll be good. I'll make him a wonderful mother." But she didn't sound serious about it.

She didn't look scared of dying.

I had my hands around her neck and my thumbs on her windpipe, but somehow I just couldn't put any pressure on. I sat there for about five minutes with the tears pouring down my face, and Jacqui lay there crying, too, with her neck in my hands.

She didn't struggle or scream or anything. I think it must have been that death wish I was talking about. People who act crazy like Jacqui act like that because deep down inside they really *want* to die. They can't face life, so they're always looking for a way out.

But I couldn't help her, I couldn't kill her. I just couldn't make myself put any pressure on her neck, I just loved her too much.

I used to wonder once how a woman could ever feel at ease, living with a man. A man's so much bigger and stronger, and if he went wild a woman could get badly hurt or killed. But a woman's usually quite safe. If a man loves her, he can't hurt her. He might be strong enough to wrestle a bear, but a little dainty woman can be as safe as houses with him because he'll never use his strength against her.

I was like that. I sat for about ten minutes with my

hands around Jacqui's neck, but I couldn't squeeze. I just sort of sank down and down until I was lying alongside her, and she put her arms around me and hugged me, and me still with my hands around her throat. And both of us had tears pouring down our faces, and we were sobbing our hearts out.

And then I killed her. I didn't know I was doing it, but I killed her.

You often read cases in the paper where people do really terrible things, things like chopping someone's head off or strangling a little kid, and their defense in court is they blacked out and didn't know what they were doing. I'd always thought, "Oh, yeah, who do you think you're kidding, mate?" I'd always thought if I was a judge I'd throw that argument straight out of court. How can anyone do something and not know they're doing it?

But it's true, you know. Once you've been through it you'll realize. If you get really screwed up, your mind just blows a fuse and you do things with no idea at all of what you're doing. You go like a lunatic just for an hour or two.

In my case, what I did was sort of fall asleep and have this terrible dream. I dreamt Jacqui had murdered our little baby, that she'd drowned him. She was in her mother's sitting room with all these dirty old men and they were all shagging her. She was standing up with no clothes on, and these guys were going in from every angle: the back, the front, the sides, in her mouth, everywhere. I was at the back of the crowd and I couldn't do anything to stop it all. But somehow I could see like an X ray of Jacqui. I could see my little baby inside her, and he was drowning. As each of the old men came his lot, it was filling up inside Jacqui and drowning my little son, the little child I loved. He was struggling to get his face out of all these sticky sperms, and I was at the back, screaming for Jacqui to stop. She heard me all right. She was looking across at me all the time and smiling as though she was really enjoying herself, and all the time my little baby was suffocating in these slimy tadpoles. They were coming right up over his face—his beautiful little face—and he was trying to get his head clear and push them away with his little hands.

I went crazy. I jumped forward and started dragging these old men away. Then Jacqui herself attacked me. She was screaming at me, spitting and scratching to drive me away so she could carry on with what she was doing. I was struggling like mad to get to the baby. Hands were grabbing me from all over the place.

Then the dream changed. Everything was quiet. Jacqui was sitting on the couch at her mother's, but it was years later. She was telling me what a wonderful person *she* was, and how inadequate *I* was, how I should reorganize my life. Inside her I could see the baby, but he was black and dead. The old men's sperms had turned into maggots and were eating him up.

"Poor Jacqui," I thought. "She's insane. She doesn't know any better."

And then I woke up. I'd gone asleep with my head on Jacqui's shoulder. I was pulling the duvet over to cover the pair of us when I saw Jacqui was dead. She must have been dead for hours, she was already starting to go stiff.

What I'd done was pull one of the pillows over her face and suffocated her. Later on, when I embalmed her, I discovered she'd choked on all the food she'd eaten. She can't have struggled much. It was almost as if she was glad to die, to be free of whatever it was tormenting her.

Chapter

6

It's a funny thing, but once Jacqui was dead I didn't feel upset anymore. In all the books and movies, you're supposed to run around in a panic feeling guilty if you kill someone. But I couldn't see anything to feel guilty about. In fact, I felt very peaceful. It was like when you have a bad dream and you wake up in the dark, and everything's black and horrible, then you fall asleep again, and when you wake up again the sun's shining and everything's peaceful and beautiful.

It seemed to me then as though Jacqui's life was something dangerous and violent, like a wild animal or a snake. While she was alive I felt frightened to death, I never knew what horrible thing she was going to do next. All the time she was alive, I was waiting for the roof to fall in on me.

But when she was dead, all the horrors just vanished. The only thing I really felt was thirsty, so I went and made a pot of tea and took it back into the bedroom to drink it. I sat on the bed beside Jacqui for hours and drank cup after cup of tea.

After a while, when the sun came up, I started thinking I'd have to get rid of Jacqui's body. I thought she might get the last laugh on me yet. The cops would be around looking for her, and if they found me with the body they'd lock me up and throw away the key. No one's got any sympathy for a bloke who strangles a girl he's got pregnant, especially when he's not married to her. They always see the girl as all innocent and helpless and the bloke as a raving sadist. They think he's done it because he's mad as hell at her for lumbering him with a kid.

People can be very stupid like that. When they're thinking of someone else's woman they forget just what sort of stinkers women can be. There's an idea goes around that women are good and men are bad. But women can be really cruel and savage, much worse than men. I read a thing once, about the Battle of Waterloo, where the Belgian women were going around after the battle castrating the French wounded lying helpless on the ground and poking their eyes out. The French lads were begging the English soldiers to shoot them in the head and give them a quick death.

Then there's that Irma Grese cow, during the war, in

Germany. She used to enjoy drowning little kids in a big muddy pit full of water. She even used to push them under with a long pole, for extra laughs. She'd hold the pole out, as though she was going to save the kids, then, when they caught hold of it, she'd push them under and pin them to the bottom.

That's what some women can be like.

Every guy you've ever met has been tortured half-insane by a woman at some time or other. I hear in America there's hardly a bloke with his balls left, the women are so predatory. What a joke it would be if I went to jail for ten years for killing Jacqui, after all the things she'd done to me.

But they could only get me if there was a body around.

Hiding Jacqui's body was the easiest bit of all, really. I can't understand why no one's thought of it before. I just rented a little flat a mile away. I was lucky with the flat. There was no landlord on the premises, so I didn't even have to make up a story, I just put Jacqui's body in the freezer, rented a van, and moved the freezer and a few clothes and bits and pieces there.

I'd wrapped Jacqui up in clean sheets and blankets and put her in the bottom part of the freezer with her clothes and shoes and handbag. The top part I filled with chops and beefburgers and ice creams so no one could see her. And after I'd taken the freezer away, I moved the furniture around in the kitchen so no one could see where it had been.

Literally the only problems I had were cleaning Jacqui up and getting the freezer in and out of the van. I don't know if you know this, but when people die they empty their bladder and bowels. I suppose it's natural enough. It just seems peculiar, somehow, that the last thing anyone should do in life is open his bowels. You could be the queen or a film star or the prime minister, but the last thing you do on earth is a job in your own underwear.

I got the freezer in the van by using the garage chain hoist to lift the front up, then shoving it in on a roller. At the other end I gave a lad a pound to help me into the flat with it. We just wheeled it into the garden, then in through the French windows.

While I was at it, I got my alibi straight. I phoned Jacqui's mother and asked to speak to her. When they said she'd gone to see me, I sounded surprised. I said I'd fallen asleep and she hadn't turned up.

I had to get my story right for the police, too. The backs of my hands were scratched where Jacqui'd been tearing at me with her nails. I guess I didn't realize she'd struggled at all. Anyway, I went straight out in the garden and started fixing the back fence. It had been falling down since the last big wind we'd had, about a month before. Of course the fence, being at the bottom of the garden, was all grown over with ivy and brambles. I got good and scratched doing it. I even got marked in the face with one thorn branch that whipped around and caught me.

The detectives turned up at the door about three weeks after Jacqui died. I'd had a couple of calls from her dad, and he'd obviously told the police she was missing. That's typical enough of crooks. They pull all kinds of stunts and dodge the law, but they don't mind a bit using the cops when it suits them.

One of the first things the tecs asked me was where I got the scratches, so I just took them straight out in the garden and showed where I'd propped the fence up. One of them got a loose thorn branch around his leg, and it clawed him through his trousers, so I got no more questions about that.

You could see they were thrown. The second I opened the door and they saw my face they must have thought "Hello, we've got him." Then, when I had my little explanations all ready, without being upset or embarrassed, it shook their confidence.

It wasn't the first time I'd been quizzed by the police. We had a to-do at the taxi office one day. Someone broke in and stole the cashbox and rifled the pay phone, and the tecs came around and questioned everyone.

It's not a bit like on television where they're barking at you with penetrating questions. "But Mr. Suspect, you said on Friday the 15th you were at *The Sound of Music,* when on that night the cinema was closed because of an IRA bomb scare. . . ." Things like that.

None of the tecs I've ever seen look a bit like Starsky and Hutch, either. They all look like tired office workers. They have on these old gabardine macs, about twenty years out-of-date, and those cheap shiny black shoes with plasticy soles. At least it shows they're honest, not taking bribes from anyone.

I felt sorry for the two who came around to my house.

It was a really wild night, with a lot of freezing rain, and they got soaked just going out to the garden. I sat them down by the fire and made them a bite to eat. I made them a pot of real coffee, and a couple of sandwiches with real ham off the bone, and a small whiskey on the side. Then I sat down with them and we just chatted. I didn't feel nervous or scared or anything. What I felt, mostly, was sorry for them.

The police have got a lousy bloody job to do. It's not their fault men and women shack up together and start trying to kill one another. But it's their job to pick up all the pieces. I'd never interfere between a man and a woman myself. I often see them on the road when I'm driving around, him glaring at her like he could kill her, and her having hysterics. No one with any sense interferes, not between a man and a woman. But the cops have got to go around after the heads have been pushed through the windows and the saucepans thrown in the faces. Or, in my case, when the woman's disappeared altogether.

They might not want to, they might think whoever got it really deserved it. But they've still got to grab you, jump all over you, and stick you away for ten or twenty years. If they didn't, there'd be bedlam. If the word once got around you could kill someone and get away with it, there'd be literally bloody murder everywhere. Practically everyone you ever meet's got someone they'd like to bump off if they thought they could get away with it. There's fellers with their women, women with their fellers, neighbors fighting over fences, blokes grabbing jobs, young people wanting old people to die so they can inherit their money, jealous lovers wanting to snuff out their rivals, people being blackmailed, you name it.

If once the law gave the word, there'd be bodies all over the streets.

But the coppers, they're only human beings like yourself, they've got the same problems as you have.

What I thought was, "Here's two mature guys, and they must be having trouble with their own women, unless they're drinkers, that is."

The older one, he looked married. I don't think he was naturally round-shouldered. His kids would be about twelve or fourteen. His wife is probably bored stiff with marriage and nags him a lot. She reads all these women's magazines that go on about having a fulfilling sex life, and she either thinks about some film star while she does it, or she's planning a little affair on the side to ginger up her union.

His eldest daughter, she's getting randy. She's painting her nails and sneaking out to pubs and discos with blokes of twenty. He'd like to take her and her mother by the hair and bang their heads together.

The younger copper isn't married yet. He's at the fiancée stage. He's been to bed with maybe three or four women, but what's itching him is his girl's been to bed with a couple of his mates. He feels he's getting second-hand goods and everyone's laughing at him, but there's nothing he can do about it, except maybe whack the girl around once he's married to her.

His life's been taken over completely by his girl friend

and her mother. They've fixed the wedding day, made up the guest list, picked the dress, chosen the honeymoon, named the kids. He hasn't had a say in anything yet. He's beginning to hate women, but he hasn't enough savvy to get off the hook.

Coppers are human, like yourself. But don't make a mistake and think you can trust them, that they'd understand. Don't get the idea that if you explained things to them, they'd help you bury the body.

You've still got to watch them. They might be human beings first, but they're still coppers second. Sometimes what they do to people is really mean and unfair. We had a driver once who was in prison, and he'd shared a cell with a guy they really shoveled it on to.

His wife was really a cow, and when he went for her one night, he ended up killing his grandmother and was sent to prison for ten years. His wife was making it with everyone in the district. One night she lay on the bed with her legs wide apart and said to him, "See that. Well, anyone in the district can have that, except you."

Jacqui did something pretty similar to me one night. She was taking off her knickers and she said, "These come off much too often. Any man who asks can get them off me."

It was very sad, really. This bloke went berserk and swung at his wife with an axe. They were in the kitchen and his grandmother jumped in the way to stop him and got killed. His life was in absolute ruins. He really loved his grandmother. She'd brought him up. He used to break down and cry every time he thought of it. And while he was doing his ten years, his wife used to send him letters telling all about the latest feller she was with and how many positions they'd tried it in.

You'd think the coppers would take things like that into account. But they don't. They still destroy a bloke's life, no matter how much he was provoked.

I wasn't going to let them put *me* in prison. That would have been the biggest travesty of justice since the courts used to jail starving children for stealing bread.

The police are your friends when you've been behaving yourself, but you do something wrong, forget to register your car, park on a yellow line, or have a body around the house, and they give you pretty short shrift.

What you've got to do in a case like that is *not* to lie your way out. The golden rule has got to be not to make up a complicated yarn. You're bound to trip yourself up. If you just say you were asleep, and stick to it, there's not a thing they can do.

The thing to remember is the cops don't have any trick questions. They just watch you all the time to see if you look flustered or frightened. But I didn't feel frightened about them finding Jacqui. In that first period, just after she died, I could hardly even remember I'd known her. She was like a vague dream to me, something that happened while you were sound asleep in bed. I felt like a guy recovering from a serious illness, everything around me seemed very calm and peaceful. It was like when you've had the flue really bad, and you come out of the fever, and everything looks transparent and very peaceful.

So, when they asked me why I hadn't missed Jacqui

when she didn't turn up, why I hadn't phoned her mother's again in the evening, I just carried on with my alibi and said I fell asleep.

"What?" they said. "At six o'clock in the evening?"

"I was pretty tired. I'd been working late all week. You lads work nights, you know what it's like."

"How come you didn't sleep during the day?"

"I'd gone past it then. I did a bit of work on that fence I showed you."

"And you slept all the evening, and the night as well?"

"I just couldn't wake up, I was absolutely shattered. Then next day I got to wondering where Jacqui had got to, so I phoned her mother."

"Didn't you think it funny she hadn't turned up?"

It was one time I was glad of Jacqui's ratbag habits, being erratic and not turning up when she'd promised. "Nah," I said, "she wasn't a bird you could ever rely on, you ask anyone."

They didn't ask me a lot of questions about Jacqui herself. The hardest one was when they said, "You must have been close, though. You bought her a wedding ring."

But I had a good answer all ready for that.

"I only bought it because she *asked* for it," I said. "You know the ideas women get sometimes?"

The younger copper nodded. We were all getting along really well.

Naturally, they asked me about the pregnancy, but I just said I was sure it wasn't mine. I was able to give them so many names of other blokes to check out that they believed me.

"She was down here with you pretty often. Why was that?"

"Ah well," I said, "every time she came I'd give her a nice meal and a fiver to take home." They nodded as though they understood very well.

One of the most useful things I said was she was a bit of a lunatic. That seemed to go home. I think if you tell any man your bird's a bit of a lunatic, he believes you. It's such a likely sort of thing, really.

They were still a little bit suspicious, of course. They asked if they could search the house and maybe put their dogs in the garden. It struck me that was a trick question. If I sounded too easy or too difficult, either would go against me. So I said, "You can if you absolutely have to, but I'd rather you didn't. What are the neighbors going to think? I've got to live here, you know. And I don't want anything damaged, holes dug or floorboards ripped up, that sort of thing."

I think that was about the best answer I could possibly have given. And not looking the least bit worried when they asked the question! I had nothing to be worried *about.* There wasn't anything they could find, it was all a mile away in the other place.

It certainly seemed to put them right off. They stopped asking questions about Jacqui and we ended up talking about the house. I practically told them my life story. They asked, Didn't I mind living in a big house on my own? I said it wasn't too bad, but I'd like to find the right woman some day and have a family.

That struck the right note, too. We were getting really friendly. They seemed two very nice lads, once they weren't being coppers. They even suggested a couple of their policewomen who might be right for me, who might like to be wives in a really nice house like mine.

We ended up our visit with a second round of sandwiches and whiskey.

They came back a couple of months later, of course, when they were getting really worried, and I asked them to search the house and grounds.

"You'd better do it," I said. "I don't intend to be under suspicion for the rest of my life."

I insisted they come around in plainclothes, in a plain van, like workmen. They brought a couple of their mates. While they tapped around in the house and poked in the garden, I made them all tea. When they went into the cellar and when they were in the most overgrown parts of the garden I made sure I was with them. I knew they were watching me, to see if I was sweating or swallowing hard, or trying to steer them around things.

I wasn't, of course. I was quite interested, in fact, to see some of the things they turned up. They went into places in the loft and cellars I'd never been myself. They found a really antique old wireless set in an oak cabinet and a Samurai sword in a leather scabbard, thick with really old grease. I cleaned both of them up later and put them on display in the front sitting room.

After that, the only one who bothered me was Jacqui's dad. He kept phoning me a long time afterward. He'd ring up about two in the morning and call me all the names under the sun.

"You know where she is, you bastard!" he'd scream. "I'll get you for this! I'll have your fucking head off!"

I just ignored him. I had no time for the likes of him. I thought if he hadn't been such a miserable little creep, his children would have grown up better. Jacqui might have been a lovely girl if he hadn't corrupted her. What chance did she stand, growing up with a guy like him? He was going about all his bent little deals, bringing all his queer mates to the house, and polluting his own children. No wonder Jacqui grew up with the idea her body was just something to be sold.

I thought once or twice he might come down with a gang and try beating me up, so I kept all the doors locked and an eye out the window. But nothing happened. He was strictly all wind.

All that time, I wasn't the least bit worried about what I'd done. For one thing, I felt positive I couldn't be caught. That makes you feel very safe and sure of yourself, when no one can catch you out.

In the movies and books, the police catch killers by finding evidence, like a dead body with a bullet in it, and the bullet's been fired from a gun licensed to the suspect, and his are the only fingerprints on the gun. All that kind of stuff.

In real life, the police depend on getting a confession.

They keep questioning you over and over till you contradict yourself. They say they know you did it, and they'll go easy on you if you confess.

But neither of those things applied to me. There was no evidence to be found, and they didn't have a story to trip me up on.

And I certainly wasn't about to confess, and put myself in prison for the best part of my life.

No one's going to spot you in the street. It doesn't show, your being a killer. I mean, you don't grow a bolt through your neck, or a hairy face and fangs. No one jumped into my taxi and went white when they caught sight of me and screamed, "Arghhh! He's a killer! I can see it in his face!" Nothing stupid like that.

The opposite happened, in one case. I picked up this woman late one night from a restaurant, and she insisted on getting in the front seat with me.

"I get so worried late at night," she said. "I even get scared in the back seat, all on me own. I feel nice and safe with a big husky lad like yourself. I can see you're a decent person, your mum brought you up well."

She wasn't trying it on. She wasn't being sexy. I mean, I'd have known, wouldn't I? She was really serious.

I always had the feeling in the back of my mind that somehow I'd done the right thing. There's millions of fellers would like to kill their woman at some time or other. She nags them, or she starts fights, or she has one-night stands with other blokes, and it drives them crazy. They would really like to murder her. Mostly though, they just shout and threaten. They might go so far as to punch her in the eye. The only difference between them and me is I went one percent further. Hardly one of *them* will give her what she deserves, hardly one of *them* will just grab her stupid neck in their hands and wring it and stop her in her tracks for good! I'm that one who did it. In a way, I feel I did it for all of them.

I saw a movie once where the hero is accused of murdering his wife. He hasn't done it really, but to get off he pretends he has. He asks the jury to let him go, because he's struck a blow for the freedom of men against nagging women. And they let him go, because they've all got wives, too, and the wives are putting them through the hoop, giving them hell and making their lives miserable. It was supposed to be only a comedy, but all the way through you could see how close it was to the truth. I struck a blow for those miserable bastards who haven't got what it takes to strangle their Jacquis.

But after a few months I started going through a bad period. There were all sorts of lonely little noises in the night I'd never noticed before, the sound of a train a long way off, a plane going by across the sky, even the fridge starting up in the kitchen. I'd lie there feeling really lost, and the darkness and the quiet all around would come creeping up on me. I'd always liked the dark before. It had seemed friendly, very deep and quiet and relaxing. But now there were times when it scared me. I'd see the sun start to set in the evening, and a kind of terror would come over me at the thought the world would soon be black and horrible. I'd switch on all the lights in the house, but somehow that wouldn't take away all the darkness. Stepping out of the house, or looking out of a window began to scare the life out of me.

Jacqui started to haunt me too. I'd be asleep in my bedroom when I'd hear a noise upstairs. It would only be the breeze making a window bump in the frame, but in my imagination it would be Jacqui coming back to get me. I'd hear her cross the landing and start coming down the stairs. I could see her face and she was scowling with that one big black eyebrow of hers and showing her teeth. I'd be really terrified. I'd think I should go upstairs and wedge the window with a bit of paper, but I couldn't have gone upstairs to save my life, not even with all the lights on.

About that time an old movie came on television about a guy who murders his lover's husband to get the insurance money. That was really a brilliant movie. Whoever wrote that understood what it was to be a killer. The average movie about killers is just rubbish. It's all "bang, bang you're dead," like little kids playing soldiers. But this old movie was brilliant. The killer's walking down this empty road at night, and he can't hear his own footsteps, and he says, "I knew I was listening to the footsteps of a dead man."

Killing someone is like that. They come back and haunt you. You try waking up at three in the morning with someone's death on your conscience. You can see their face in the dark, and they're looking at you and saying, "Why did you do it?"

I read a thing, too, about the guards in concentration camps, and how they could only kill people for so long, and then their nerve went. The Germans were the best killers, because they were the steadiest and could go on longest. The Nazis tried just about everybody else in Europe for doing the job. The Hungarians and the Rumanians were the most brutal, they really enjoyed gassing and burning people. But they would only last about two months before they had a nervous breakdown and couldn't do it anymore. Even the ones who could keep killing went half-mad. Nighttime's a horrible time for killers. The Jerry guards used to have to get drunk out of their minds before they could sleep, and even then they'd wake up screaming with terrible nightmares.

I felt like that, having killed Jacqui. I felt like a sort of leper among other people, an alien, someone from another planet. I kept on looking at all these other people as they passed me in the street, and all the time I kept saying to myself, "You've killed someone. You've got blood on your hands. You've taken another human being's life."

And I'd look at all these other people, and think the other way around, "They're normal, they haven't killed anyone. Not like me."

I saw in their faces that some of them were worried. Perhaps they were behind with the rent, or they'd lost a week's wages on the horses, or maybe they'd even just been told they had a year to live with cancer. But I felt, "It doesn't matter what it is, mate. If you haven't killed anyone, you don't know the meaning of the word worry."

I worried that Jacqui's father and sister might think of something to tell the cops that would bring them around again with more questions. I'd done so well the first time, but my energy was down these days.

One time when I was at my lowest, I even tried curb crawling. I was driving back from a job at the airport late one night and I thought I was going to *die* of misery. I'd taken a young couple who were off on a winter break holiday in Spain, and I could hardly bear to let them go. I had the feeling that if they got out of the car and left me on my own, the night would swallow me up.

When you're really unhappy, the night can seem like a huge black animal that's growling around trying to eat you.

I felt like that. When I drove away from the airport lights and down dark roads, I felt I was driving straight toward the tonsils of this enormous mouth. The roads were all wet where it had been raining, and it was just like I was sliding down this huge wet black throat.

And then I passed this bus stop with a girl standing at it, and the idea came to me to try and pick her up. I thought, "If only I had a nice girl to talk to, to have her put her arms around me, I'd feel safe." The girl at the bus stop looked really sweet and kind.

I did a U turn about a mile up the road, came past the girl again, and turned around again another mile away where she couldn't see me. Then I pulled up at the bus stop and asked her the way. I'd spilled all my maps over the seat to make it look realistic. When she told me the way, I tried to pick her up.

I was writhing inside myself with what I was doing, but I couldn't seem to help it.

She was a really nice-looking girl, very sweet and kind looking. Maybe if I'd just told her I was feeling low, she'd have understood.

She went all worried looking. She said "No" in a really nice way, she said she couldn't do that.

I wish I'd known her address, so I could have sent her a bunch of flowers, for being such a nice person.

That's what I needed, a nice person. Maybe someone I could love enough to give a ring to.

The ordinary bloke looking for a nice, loving person drives around in his car, and cars can make a woman suspicious, can't they? But I had my taxi, and some people, maybe because they've taken taxis now and again, they aren't so suspicious. I had a plan to drive around more, increase my chances. That made me feel better.

Chapter

7

It was around that time I nearly turned religious. I was never brought up to go to church. My mother said it was all a load of rubbish. Yet now I started praying to God. You know this feeling you get about God, you think if only you believe in Him and pray to Him, He'll help you and look after you?

A lot of times in life you can get really scared of all the things that could happen to you, getting crippled, dying, losing your wife and children, all that sort of thing. And then you think if maybe God was on your side He'd protect you. He'd be up there looking after you. I got the feeling I was hemmed in by all this danger, nosy neighbors, coppers, judges and things, but if I prayed to God, He'd help me and keep me safe from them all and maybe even help me find a nice woman.

I kept saying to myself, "Oh God, help me, please help me, God," just as though He could hear me. I'd drive along the road muttering it to myself. If God helped me find a nice woman, someone I could talk to. Then I realized what I was up to.

I had got this terrible craving to tell someone what I'd done. I kept saying to myself, "You're mad. You're crazy. You'll end up in jail for the rest of your life."

But I couldn't help it. I was like an addict looking for a fix. I felt I was going to burst if I didn't talk about it to someone. I'd even have people in the taxi, just strangers, and I'd get this urge to turn around and just say to them I was a killer. You could just imagine their faces, at one in the morning down some dark road.

I ended up nearly blabbing to a couple of blokes who came around to the house selling religion.

One evening about eight the doorbell rang. I was feeling really bad just then. The house was scaring the life out of me. I was dreading the night taking over the house, yet I was too slack somehow to get the car out and go taxiing instead. I was just sitting in front of the television driving myself around the bend.

When I went to the door, I found two religious guys on the step. You could tell they were selling religion the second you saw them, they both looked very calm and clean and well dressed. That's something you can envy in religious people, they often look very peaceful in themselves. The average guy who's not religious usually looks very screwed up, as though he's got a thousand problems on his mind. But religious people often look as though they haven't a care in the world, as though they're really enjoying life.

I asked them in. Usually I just chase them, I can't stand Holy Joes waving bibles at me. I get the feeling they're just high on religion, ignoring reality and living on dreams. Either that, or they're really hard-nosed money-makers who milk the faithful and live in big style themselves.

But that night I invited them in.

Of course they spotted the state I was in right away. Religious door knockers thrive on peoples's grief. If a guy's healthy and happy and they knock on his door, he just tells them he's got everything he needs. But they get their foot inside with lonely people, and widows, and people in trouble like myself. They scent blood if you call them inside the minute they say who they are.

They really gave *me* the works. They had a projector with them, and they showed me a movie all about how much God loves you. It was full of soulful music and heavenly choirs and pretty girls.

There was no mention of anything about real life, about everything eating everything else, and little children being run over, and millions of people dying every year of disease. Maybe they thought God wasn't in charge of that bit, He only organized the good side of life.

It was just pure schmaltz, really. It was like a cornflake ad on television. They were just selling a product. They must have spent months working out camera angles and putting the soundtrack together, and I was the sucker who was supposed to buy it.

I damned near did. I was ashamed of myself afterward, but at the time I was having to grit my teeth to stop from bursting into tears.

They could see they were getting through to me, they could see I was bursting to tell them something. They kept saying to me, "Is there something you want to confess, brother? Is there something you want to say to the Lord? Let us confess together."

They opened their briefcases and took out a bunch of magazines. I thought they were going to show them to me, but they put them on the carpet and knelt on them. The magazines were just for kneeling on, to keep fluff and hairs off their trousers. They didn't offer *me* one. Maybe they thought sinners didn't mind getting fluff and hairs on their trousers. They hitched up their trousers and knelt down on these magazines in front of the fire, then sat back on their heels waiting for me to join them.

It seemed such a beautiful thing to do. I thought, "I'll pour it all out and I'll feel so much better." You hear about people walking into police stations and owning up to things they've done twenty or thirty years before. They just can't live with themselves, with the guilt.

I had a sort of vision of myself driving the two of them around to the flat, opening the door, taking them into the kitchen. I could see their faces as I lifted the lid on the freezer and unwrapped Jacqui.

This really weird feeling came over me. I felt myself

being pushed toward the ground, as though two big hands were pressing a huge load of guilt onto my shoulders.

But something warned me just in time. I caught a look in their eyes. They were sort of gloating. They were trying to look holy, as though they were praying, but I could see this gloating look in their eyes. I thought, "These bastards will snitch on me. If I tell them what's happened, they'll be off to the law like a rocket. The little creeps will be happy to get their names in the paper and get a bit of free publicity for their religion."

Either that, or they'd milk me for every penny I had. Once they had the goods on me, they could rip me right off. I'd probably end up with my house as one of their temples. They'd throw all the good books out of the library and stuff it full of pamphlets and tracts

I pulled back just in time. Boy, was that a close one! Instead of telling them what I'd done and putting my head in a noose, I offered them a cup of tea. But they wouldn't have it. Nor coffee, nor whiskey, nor wine, nor beer, nor anything but a glass of water. When they'd finished their glass of water, I told them I had to be going out to work. The older one said, "Would you like us to call back another day?"

"No," I said. "I'm not interested."

They were livid. They went away absolutely furious. If looks could kill, I'd have turned up my toes in the hall. Was I glad I'd kept my mouth shut! Fancy people like that having the goods on you!

I got the whole thing off my chest one evening later on. There was a movie on TV one night where the killer goes to a priest in church, and the next thing I knew I'd gone in one myself and was sitting in a corner at the back.

I didn't know what to do. I felt like the old man of ninety-seven who went to confession because he'd got a girl of sixteen in the family way.

"My God," the priest asked him, "is the young lady a Catholic?"

"No, Father," says the old boy, "and neither am I."

"Then what are you telling me all this for?"

"Father," says the old boy, "I'm telling everyone."

After a while I noticed people coming and going into a confessional box nearby. They'd come up very quietly, go inside for a couple of minutes, then come out again and go off somewhere else in the church to say their prayers. When they were inside, you couldn't hear a word they were saying, not a whisper. I really felt it would be safe to go in there and spill the beans.

I waited till there was no one else around, till the church was empty. I didn't want some bloke waiting outside for me to finish, I was going to take the better part of an hour.

You couldn't see the priest inside. There was a sort of partition in between us, and it was pitch-dark. He sounded like an old man, very kind, with a very soft voice. He kept saying things that had the tears pouring down my face. I told him everything about Jacqui, why I strangled her, that I still had the body and all.

I was really desperately sorry. I wanted him to tell me God forgave me. He did. All the time I was telling him what happened he kept saying, "There now, God forgives

170

you. You're His little child and He loves you and forgives you."

Every time he said that, he had me in floods. I could hardly breathe for all the tears running in my mouth. I was thinking he was the nicest old man I'd ever met in my life.

But at the end, he spoiled it. You know what he said when I'd finished? You'll never guess? He said I should give myself up to the law. He said, "There now, you've made a good confession. Now I think what you should do is go along to the police and tell them what you've just told me."

I was amazed. What a stupid thing to say! I'd poured my heart out to him, and then he goes and says something stupid like "Go to the police."

You go to a man who's supposed to be dealing with the next world, and he tells you to go to an organization like the police, whose chief concern is protecting money and property in this world. All the police would do is put you in a squalid bloody prison cell and keep you locked up till your heart and mind were completely destroyed.

I got out of there double-quick in case he got the idea to call the law on me. As I went down the aisle, I kept my hand over my face in case he was peeping through his curtains to see what I looked like and maybe finger me later on.

Despite the priest's ridiculous suggestion, I felt much better afterward. I stopped being haunted in the night. And the bursting to tell other people what I'd done left me. If God was going to forgive me, He'd forgive me. I didn't need a second opinion from any other silly bugger, just because he was wearing a dog collar or waving a bible around. The thing is, you don't need to go to anyone else for religion, you can make up your own. Every man ought to have a religion that suits him. What suited me was the confession part. I didn't have the craving to tell anyone anymore. I was free.

The only thing I had to worry about was being caught with the body.

Chapter

It's a weird feeling, being stuck with the body of someone you've killed. Till you've got one, you don't realize what a huge great lump of material it is. It's heavier than a bag of cement, and harder to hide than an erection in a swimsuit.

It's no good to anyone. It's disgusting, in fact. People would pay you to take it away and get rid of it. But if you get caught with it, you might just as well count your life finished.

And it would be just so easy, getting caught with it. I kept imagining all the thousands of things that could go wrong at the small flat I'd rented. The freezer might break down. There might be a fire, or a flood, or a break-in.

If anything at all like that happens to your place, the police come along and search everything. They say they're just making sure your property's safe, but they're looking for things to nail you with as well.

They did that once with one of the lads at work. He had a fire in his flat (he went out and left his electric blanket on, all crumpled up), and the police searched the place and found a live bullet on his mantlepiece and took him to court.

This lad, Bill, couldn't even remember where he got it from. You know how people just give you a bullet sometimes, and you think it must be a blank and you put it in your pocket? But they took him to court: magistrates, lawyers, wigs, gowns, the whole pantomime, and they fined him one whole week's wages, just for having the thing.

And they tagged him with a criminal record too— "illegal possession of explosives"—the same as if he'd had as much gunpowder as Guy Fawkes. So, if they did that to him over one lousy cartridge, just think what they'd do to me.

I found myself going around to the small flat every other day. Everything was always just as I'd left it, but then I'd come home and have nightmares about the police finding the body and tracing it back to me. It was *my* freezer with *my* fingerprints all over it. And there were neighbors who'd identify me as the tenant. I'd always parked my car in the next road and walked around to the flat, but you could bet there'd be *some* nosy sod who knew all my movements.

It worried me so much I decided to give the flat up and move everything back home. I put the freezer back in the kitchen while I tried to think of ways of getting rid of the body. I read all these books on forensic science, and how different people used different ways to get rid of people they'd killed.

Burial's the first one you think of, and the first one you decide against. The problem with burying a body is that you've got nowhere to bury it except the little piece of ground you live on, and that's the first place the police always look. Even if they'd already dug at it once, like with me, they could always come back for another try. You'd have to live with the fear of that all the time. And of the body being found accidentally. Every time you saw a cat scratching in the garden, you'd have heart failure. And you could never move or go on holiday.

There's an excellent book about that, called *Payment Deferred,* about a guy who plants a corpse in his own garden, and first it drives him mad, and then it kills him. So, don't stick a body in your own patch, find somewhere else.

Except your own garden, you've only got public ground to use, and bodies buried in scenic spots and golf courses are always found inside a couple of months. There's just so many people go there, and every second one of them's got a dog, cocking its leg up all over the place and shoving its nose into everything.

The next thing you think of is the sea. You imagine the

dark ocean depths swallowing the thing up forever. But, do you know, it's a hell of a job just getting *near* the sea?

I spent a whole Sunday going miles along the coast looking for the right sort of place. Ninety-nine percent of the coast is built up, with bungalows and boatyards and things. The places left are real public, like you've got to drive down the High Street of some seaside town, and when you finally do get to water there's about a million people milling around eating ice creams and fish and chips. You could just imagine staggering down there with a body, past all the amusement arcades and deckchairs.

I drove nearly two hundred miles that day and didn't find a single place that was practical. Things always get washed up from the sea anyway. One bloke I read of hired a plane and dropped the body in the middle of the English Channel, but it still got washed up, and he went to prison for about twenty years.

You'd think the fishes would eat the things, but they don't. Maybe there aren't any fish left anymore and it's all plastic bottles and oil slicks. Or maybe they're all hooked on eating raw sewage and don't know a good meal when they see one.

There are a whole lot of weird ways of getting rid of a corpse. One guy I read about took it to a country cottage and lived off it for months, they said, though I don't know how true that was. He's supposed to have taken a whole caseful of tomato sauce to help it down.

Then there was a woman got kidnapped and was never seen again, and they reckon she was fed to the pigs on a farm. That could be true, porkers have got jaws like boa constrictors.

Around that time too, there was this guy up for murder. He got rid of the body in the living room fire. He just burned it up piece by piece. He spread a big sheet of polythene on the carpet in front of the fire, then he just carved the body up lump by lump and burned it to nothing. It took him a week to do it, but no one got suspicious, and there wasn't a trace of the thing left. The only reason he owned up was he was caught for something else and was making a clean breast of everything.

The difference between him and me was he killed someone who hadn't done him any harm, so he got a conscience about it.

I thought about using his technique on Jacqui but I knew I couldn't bear the thought of cutting her up and burning her. You could maybe manage the legs and arms and things, but could you imagine how you'd feel when you got to the head?

I could see Jacqui's head in all these hot coals, and it frightened the life out of me. Her hair would go up first, of course. There'd be a big "fizz," and a cloud of sparks, and there'd be a big singeing smell. Then the heat would start to get at her skin and that would peel off and splutter when the fat melted.

The lad at the firm, Bill, who was fined for having the bullet, he worked in a crematorium once, and through a peephole in the oven, he used to watch the corpses burn. It was really grotesque. He said if you could ever watch a cremation, you'd never agree to have it done to yourself. Or to anyone you liked.

The body goes mad when the heat gets to it. It tries to jump up off the slab. You get the feeling it's writhing in agony. Of course, it's just the tendons and things shrinking, but the arms and legs flap around and the backbone bends to the shape of a bow.

And all the time this is happening, the heat's scorching the skin off, and the fat's melting down in rivers. Especially if it's someone with a heavy build, a big booze-and-fags man, or one of those women who's always at the cream cakes. There's a lot of blubber on them. You could fill a lot of frying pans off someone like that.

And then comes the really gorgeous bit: you just swell up and burst. The eyes go first. They just shoot out of your head, like two boiled eggs going into orbit, and splatter on the steel plate above. Then the rest of you goes to smithereens all over the place, in more bits than a car windshield when a brick hits it.

I decided not to burn her. I thought I'd never sleep again for the rest of my life with that on my mind. I thought about dissolving her in acid instead. She'd just turn to sludge and go down the drain. That's how Haigh did it. He lured middle-aged women to a little factory he had down in Sussex, then dissolved them in a big tank of acid. He got caught because all the women were big fatties who were always stuffing themselves with cream cakes, and women like that have gallstones that don't dissolve.

I went to a couple of pharmacies and asked about

sulfuric acid. I said I wanted it for a chemistry set. I was told you can't have more than a thimbleful. Apparently you've only got to add it to garden fertilizer and it makes dynamite, and this was during the time the IRA were letting off bombs all over the country.

I was glad in a way, the idea was giving me the horrors. Could you imagine putting someone in a batch of acid and watching them dissolve? They'd melt like soap in a dish. Every day they'd get blurrier and blurrier. The face would all fall in and the fat and muscle slide off the bones. After a while there'd just be a skeleton, surrounded by a sea of jelly, and then it would all crumble to nothing and you could just stir it with a stick.

All except the teeth. They'd still be grinning at you a week later.

I finally decided that the best way to get rid of any body was to put it in the meat system. By the "meat system," I mean all the butcher shops and slaughterhouses and sausage works and meat-pie factories, all that sort of thing. There's eyes and brains and hearts and guts and lungs and livers all over the place. Who'd notice the odd human body among that lot? Sweeney Todd got away with it for years. He only got caught because he left fingernails in the meat pies.

Old Sweeney, he ran a barber's shop, and if a strange customer came in (someone who'd never been in the district before and no one knew was there), Sweeney used to cut his throat and make meat pies out of him. He had a special barber's chair that turned upside down and dumped the body in the cellar under the shop. He'd be shaving away, chatting, and "zip!" you'd be in the cellar like a flash, with your jugular cut. He'd nip down afterward and rob the body. Then he'd get rid of it in his own meat-pie factory next door.

No one noticed. Human meat's very like any other. If it's a crime to kill a human being, then it should be a crime to kill a lamb or a calf as well, they're just the same as us.

Even the customer would benefit. He'd get much more good meat in his pie with a young girl's body in it than he ever would with all the old rubbish they usually use. Some of the manufacturers mush up snouts and ears and gristle and testicles and cockroaches and everything to make their pies and hotdogs.

The police have an official missing list of thousands of people who've just vanished from the face of the earth, and it stands to reason some of them ended up like that. I'll bet there must be stacks of people ended up as sizzling sausages.

I thought of all those things, but I couldn't do any of them. I had to stop. I felt I'd go around the bend if I carried on thinking like that. My head seemed to be splitting all the time.

I finally got to thinking of killing myself again. That seemed the best thing of all, in fact. What difference does it make if you die now, or in fifty years' time? I went around thinking about death. It made everything seem so simple.

People drive themselves mad trying to solve their problems. They work themselves into a breakdown to get more money, they worry about their families, their houses, their cars. You even get some nutters worry about things like pets, they get all choked up if the parakeet dies.

Yet there isn't a single problem in life that can't be solved simply by dying.

Suppose you're in the sort of mess I was, with a dead body around the house. If you were alive, the coppers and judges could torture you by locking you up in a little cell for years and years. But if you're dead you can laugh at them all. They can't hurt a corpse.

Chapter

I'm not the sort of man to let things get me down forever. You either have to forget your troubles in this life, or they kill you. You can have a thing like a deep freeze in your kitchen with a body in it, and you can forget all about it. If a thing gets you down too much you just put it out of your mind. I even started using the freezer again. I had the top part full of quick snacks like beefburgers and chicken legs, and when I was hungry I'd dip in the freezer for one to fry up. Often enough I could do that without even thinking of Jacqui being there, just under the baskets. You couldn't see her, because she was all wrapped up in blankets and sheets. All you could see was a whiteness at the bottom of the freezer.

It was sad, really. I could feel my love for Jacqui dying. You think when you love someone madly, when you're really crazy about them, that there'll never come a time when it's hard even to keep your mind on them, to think about them for more than a few seconds.

But sooner or later the time comes. I never thought there'd be a time when I wouldn't grieve about Jacqui and my little baby, but one day I was driving down the road and I started thinking about them, and I realized I hadn't thought about them for days. If you get cut off long enough from someone, that's how you feel. You get so you couldn't care less about them, it's just human nature. It was all very sad. I could have been a good husband and father. I think I could have made Jacqui very happy, if she'd have let me. And I could have loved that child tremendously. I could have worshipped that kid. But his mother had made it all impossible.

I found it was easier to think of other things. I started thinking of all the things I'd been missing. The world was full of thousands of beautiful girls, and I was crying over a corpse. I'd had the usual number of offers during this time, but I'd turned them all down.

For some reason I didn't fancy just making it with one girl and going through the old routine.

I thought perhaps what had gone wrong was I'd been too much of a loner for years.

If there's one person you should envy in this life it's the happy-go-lucky type. He mightn't have a penny to his name, but he's always whistling and singing. That's because he doesn't get attached to anything. He wraps his car around a lamp post and laughs like a bullfrog. "It's just a car," he says. "I can always get another."

Another guy would be crying his eyes out, seeing his radiator smashed in and his oil running down the gutter.

Or he's got a girl friend, and she goes off and leaves him, so he just shrugs, and the next thing he's going around with another girl twice as nice.

A bloke like that attracts good luck. Everyone likes him because he's cheerful and a good sort.

The worst thing you can be in life is serious over anything. What's a thing worth, if having it makes you miserable? What's the good of having a nice house, car, wife, kids, anything, if you're all the time fretting over it? A change in life-style might do me good.

If I hadn't worried about Jacqui, if I'd wished her fair wind to her backside, I'd be having a good time, instead of fretting my guts out. I'd been too screwed up by half. I'd never really had any fun all my life. I'd lived all alone in a big house, looking after it, digging in the garden, working on the car. Yes, definitely, what I needed was a change.

I thought what I'd do was turn myself into a *bon viveur*. You know, the sort of guy who's got stacks of friends. I could see the picture, me in my big house, and all these people just dropping in for a chat all the time. I'd have lots of girl friends, two or three at a time, so I wouldn't get stuck on just the one and give myself problems. I'd take life very lightly.

I decided to start off my new life-style by giving a party. That way I could get to know a lot of people, girls and things. It seems there's a sort of circuit with these things.

All the people who go to parties have got like a grapevine. They've always got their ear to the ground. You contact one and you've contacted them all.

This bloke, Tony, at the taxi office, started the ball rolling. He was a great partygoer. I happened to mention "party" in front of him and he took me up on it like a shot. How I could ever have gotten the idea *he* was going to improve my life, I can't imagine. He was a cheerful sort of bloke in some ways, he could make you laugh, but that apart, he was always going on about people being unfair to him. He was one of those guys who always blames his parents for everything that is wrong with his life. Twenty-seven years of age, and he was still blaming his mother for his troubles.

But he said he'd arrange the party, get people to come and everything.

You'll never believe what I did, for my part. It sounds incredibly stupid now, but I cleaned the whole house up to be ready for my guests. I vacuumed the place right through, cleaned the two sitting rooms, downstairs bathroom, kitchen, dining room, hall, stairs. I even cleaned the windows and polished the mirrors.

Then I drove down to a delicatessen and spent a wad of money on sliced ham and cheeses and crispy rolls and things. I put all this on plates and laid the big table in the hall with a cloth and put everything on it.

If only I'd known what was going to happen.

First of all, Tony turned up with this mate of his, George. They had a load of paraphernalia in the boot of the car, a sort of seduction kit. There was the record player, the speakers, and a stack of records. Then they brought in a big box full of red light bulbs and started screwing them in all the sockets. They took the ordinary bulbs out and put in these red things that made the place look as if it was on fire.

I should have realized what I was in for when I saw the way they were treating my furniture. They thought nothing of standing on a polished table or a tapestried chair with their shoes on, just to get their seduction lamps plugged in.

They had this look in their eyes barflies get when there's a party coming up. Tony usually spent half his time whining, and George was normally a miserable sod. But they'd gone really cheerful. I found out why afterward: they'd promised themselves all sorts of screwing at my expense.

I felt even more nervous when the guests started to arrive. They were all crazies. You know, the sort of people who've got to be at parties eight nights a week or they get depressed and commit suicide? They never read a book or dig in the garden or anything useful. They spend all their time dressing themselves up and going out. They usually live in squalor. I went around to Tony's place once, and it was just a smelly, tiny flat, where he lived on tea and digestive biscuits.

The first thing they did was turn up the record player till the plaster was showering off the ceilings. Then they all lit up about three cigarettes apiece and started puffing like mad, till you couldn't see across the room and you had to breathe in installments.

Once they got the atmosphere right, they all started trying to screw one another. All the blokes were trying to get off with the good-looking girls and ignoring the ugly ones, and all the girls were doing the same with the blokes.

The kitchen was like a battlefield. Everyone had brought a bottle, wrapped in tissue paper. When you took the paper off, you could see why it was wrapped. Half of it was cider, or dead cheap wine. They all dumped their bottles of rubbish, then poured themselves big glasses of my spirits.

Somehow or other I ended up with a bunch of three French girls in a corner of the back sitting room. They were trying to chat me up, sit on my lap, all that sort of thing. But I couldn't relax. I was a bundle of nerves with the way everyone was carrying on.

Just the smoking made me wild. I don't like smoking in my house. It's a dirty, destructive habit. You can't have a decent home when there's a smoker around. Everything stinks. And everything gets burned: table tops, carpets, bed covers, windowsills.

You go in two compartments on a train, one a smoker and one not, and you'll see what I mean. The smoker compartment is like a dustbin. And the people in it are different, they're a dirty decrepit-looking lot compared with the nonsmokers.

Smokers are such selfish pigs. If you say to one of them, "Don't put your lit cigarette down on that polished table, it's a valuable antique," he says back, "Oh, don't be such an old woman, carrying on about an old table." As though his grotty little obsession with sucking smoke up his nose is more important than really beautiful craftsman-made furniture.

No one at the party was respecting my property at all. I could see them putting lit cigarettes down on polished tables and on the arms of chairs. When they couldn't find an ashtray, they just dropped the lit ends and trod them into the carpets or the floors I'd just polished.

And then some of them started on drugs. You get people who don't mind poisoning themselves with tobacco smoke, they don't mind poisoning themselves with everything else as well. Tranquilizers, pot, horse, aspirin, uppers, downers, glue, metal polish, meths! They'd eat dog shit if they thought they could get a thrill out of it.

One of the French girls I was with was crunching up these little white tablets, and after a while she started acting like a lunatic. She was screeching and laughing, and every now and then she'd collapse all over me. I got really worried about her.

"Look," I said to her mates, "I'd better get her on a bus home."

I took her out the back way, through the French windows. We were sitting right up against them, so it was easy just to slip out the back. To go out the front door would have meant pushing through all the crowd, and everyone would have been asking what was up. I led her across the lawn and around the house to the front drive. She was laughing all the time in this really maniac way. If I shushed her, she just made a louder noise. And then, right in the middle of the pavement, she just hiked her skirt up and squatted down to piss in the road, like a cart horse.

Was *I* glad to get her on a bus and see the back of her.

When I got back to the house, I went in the front way. Someone had stuck about six big notices all along the fence saying "PARTY HERE." I tore them down. The door was wide open, so I locked it. Anyone could have just walked in off the street. I could have had everything stolen from the house, but nobody cared.

Inside the house, the screwing had started. On the couches, behind the couches, on the window seats, in the armchairs. Most of the blokes still had their shoes on, on my tapestried furniture, and at least one of them was really digging his toes in. I went in the ground-floor bedroom and chucked out a bloke who was screwing a bird in my bed, then had to go upstairs and lock all the other bedrooms, or I'd have been laundering sheets and bedspreads for a week.

When I went back to where I'd left the French girls, Tony was waiting for me.

"Where's that other French bird?" he asked me as soon as I turned up, and when I said I'd put her on a bus he started looking all worried.

"George'll go crazy," he said. "He had her lined up to shag her tonight. He used all his dope up on her. He was looking for her just now, and the other girls said you'd taken her out the back. He's been prowling around in the garden looking for you."

Then he said, "You didn't shag her yourself, did you?"

I thought at first he must be joking, then I realized how big a difference there was between my sort and his sort. The thought of having it off with that coarse, drunken Frenchwoman made me feel sick. The likes of Tony and George could get a thrill out of a thing like that, poking some stupid bird out of her mind with drink and drugs.

"Anyway," Tony said, "you'd better watch out. George is in a vicious mood."

So we were going to have a fight, too. Booze parties are like weddings, they're never complete without a brawl.

I had a nose-to-nose with George a couple of minutes later. He was livid about his Frenchwoman getting away, but he was too yellow to do anything. He stood there muttering threats, with all his mates behind him, and I just faced him and waited for him to start something. If he'd pulled any stunts, I'd have whacked his teeth so far down his throat he'd have had to shove his toothbrush up his anus to clean them.

I was starting to get mad by then. But I was more mad with myself than with anyone else. I was thinking, "What sort of a bloody lunatic were you, letting this bunch of jerks into your house?"

I did nothing after that but go around the house trying to keep the damage down. I caught one bunch trying to phone Australia. I was going to have a phone bill that would buy me a new car, so I went outside and unscrewed the wires from the central box. Then I stood near the front door and closed it about five hundred times as people kept leaving it open.

Next, I went around all the rooms picking up my

valuable ornaments and locking them in my bedroom. Some silly sod was swinging the Samurai sword around so I took it off him and locked that away, too.

I heard a commotion from the kitchen. There was smoke pouring out of the door. Someone had put a frying pan on a high gas, and the oil was nearly on fire. I dashed in there. About twenty people were milling around, trying to make themselves a snack. They'd wolfed all the food from the buffet, and now they'd invaded the kitchen. Worst of all, someone had forced the freezer open. I'd been very careful to lock that and to put a load of jars and boxes all over the lid so no one would touch it. But someone had forced the lock, and now about a dozen of them were rooting around inside for beefburgers and chicken legs.

I felt really sick when I saw that. I felt as though I'd dragged Jacqui and myself in the dirt by opening the door to all these squalid little buggers. They'd dirtied our home, they'd stubbed their filthy cigarette ends out on our furniture, they'd tried shagging one another in our bed, and now they were rooting around with their stinking drunken fingers just a few inches from Jacqui's face. And her not able to lift a finger to help herself.

I went dead icy inside. I really went terrible. I just wanted to get my place clear of these scum. I grabbed the lid of the freezer and brought it down as hard as I could on all the hands and arms trying to dig out the food. It didn't work as well as I'd hoped—I'd thought it would come smashing down and break all their fingers. I thought I'd have been happy to see them all writhing on the floor with their hands broken. But the lid was only light plastic or something, and there were about ten of them with their arms and shoulders inside. It just sort of bounced off them all without doing anyone any real harm.

I realized afterward how lucky I'd been. If anyone had been hurt, the police would have been around holding an inquest around the freezer.

But it got through to them, they all sort of stopped. The only thing moving was the smoke coming up from the frying pan. I went over and switched the gas off. Then I switched the kitchen fan on and turned around on this lot. I was really expecting a fight. I thought someone was going to take a swing at me for banging the freezer lid down on him, but they were just all sort of milling around rubbing their shoulders and arms. They really were a putrid lot. They must have known what I was going to say, but I said it anyhow. I wasn't rude or foulmouthed or anything, I just said, "You'd better go now, the party's over."

You know how it is, if you're in the right you feel miles stronger than even a big mob of people. I felt I was defending my family. I saw a war memorial once on a village green, from the First World War. The First World War memorials are always completely different from the Second. The Second World War only ever has lists of names, while the First has these really noble statues. In this memorial I remember, the soldier is holding his rifle and standing in front of a young mother and her baby to protect them. He's already been wounded. He's got this big bandage around his arm, but he's standing there dead grim facing the enemy and protecting his wife and child.

That's the way I felt in the kitchen, standing there facing that mob. More of them were pushing in through the door. They could smell a fight. But the more of them came in, the better I felt.

I guess it was the determination on my face that convinced them. They all just backed down and left. I heard a few mutters of "lunatic," but I didn't care. I just wanted the lot of them out of my house.

It took me hours to clean up the mess. I vacuumed up about a bucketful of fag ends and other rubbish, and I had to leave all the windows open for a week to get rid of the stink. The bathroom carpet had to be thrown away, too, where drunken people had missed, and pissed all over it.

And all the time I was setting things right, I was thinking about Jacqui. I was thinking, "Whatever else, she's sort of like my wife. If I haven't got her, then I haven't got anybody. She's mine, for better or worse."

When I got the place a bit straight, I went and had a look at her. It was about three in the morning. I locked the kitchen doors and drew the curtains at the windows, then cleared all the stuff away from her and unwrapped her sheets.

It's a funny thing, but when I did that I felt I loved her. I know she'd done all those horrible things when she was alive, but when someone's dead you find it hard to think anything bad of them. No one ever says on the memorial that the soldiers who died were ordinary blokes, that some of them were yellow, some thieves, some would have raped their own granny. And no one says any of them died shot up the backside while they were running away, or blew their own brains out because they were too frightened to go over the top. They're dead, so they're all beautiful young lads forevermore. All you'll ever think of them is like the statue on the plinth, the wounded soldier giving his life for his country.

That was how I felt about Jacqui. When she was alive, it was like sharing your life with a stupid animal. It was like having a mule to live in the house and trying to share your living quarters with it. You can imagine the mess, having a mule in your kitchen, barging things over, never cleaning anything up.

But once she was dead a while, I couldn't even think those bad things about her. They were true, they'd all happened, but they didn't even want to come into my mind. Other thoughts came instead, things I'd almost forgotten had ever happened. I started remembering a time we went for a walk along the road and I picked a little snowdrop growing on the edge of someone's garden, and Jacqui was really hurt. "Oh," she'd said, "how mean! Now you've killed the poor little thing," and she was really upset. She wasn't putting me on or pretending, she really was hurt by my picking that flower.

And the thing was, she made *me* feel what a wrong thing I'd done. I'd always liked snowdrops, I'd always looked on them as my own flower, because I was born in January, but Jacqui made me see how wrong it was just to pluck them and kill them.

"It was just enjoying its little life there," she said, "and you come along and break off its little head, and now it will die."

I remember looking at the snowdrop and feeling like a criminal, and I looked at her and she looked really beautiful and hurt, with little tears in her eyes.

And another time Jacqui was with me when I was driving, and we picked up this really neurotic woman who wouldn't stop talking about her troubles. She drove me mad, but Jacqui was really patient and kind with her. We ended up sitting for two hours in her house, drinking tea and listening about her husband who'd run off on her about twenty years before. Jacqui was really kind and nice with her.

I was watching her while the woman talked, and she had this very motherly, very gentle look about her.

She did spoil it a little bit by eating this huge great chocolate cake the woman put in front of us. I think she only meant us to have a slice each, but Jacqui sort of quietly ate the lot, and the woman was so busy talking she didn't seem to notice.

The thing was, Jacqui wasn't so bad. For a start, she was miles better than those party-going lunatics I'd had in the house. She didn't go smoking her face off and getting drunk every night, she was much more decent than that.

And she wasn't a money grubber, like a lot of women are. She could have had my big house for the asking, but she turned it down. How many women would have done that? The average woman would have moved in with her mother and family and taken me over.

You get those money-grubbing women, they're much worse than Jacqui ever was. They're hard and mean. You drop them off at their houses sometimes and they never give you a tip. They'll hardly give you the time of day. They've got these massive big houses with gardens you could set up a row of party tents in, and they won't even give a taxi driver a ten-penny tip. They haven't even got the decency to be ashamed of themselves. When they're paying you, they hold every twopence piece up to the light to make sure it's not a five.

They're usually very classy looking themselves, good legs, a stack of cash on their backs, but they marry these really ugly little guys just for their money. I'd be ashamed to be seen on the road with them if I was a woman. They've got greasy black hair with a great big egg in the nest, and they've usually got the sort of breath you could use for stripping paint. At least Jacqui didn't stoop to that.

And then, how many women are much more decent than Jacqui on the sex side? There's millions of them cheat on their husbands and kids just like she did, but they're not honest enough to own up.

On the way back from long trips, I often turn into parks or scenic spots for a cup of tea or a bit of fresh air and quiet, and you see that sort of thing all the time. You've stopped there for a little break, and you see a woman in another car near you. She looks really nervous, and she's all the time looking at her watch. Then another car drives up with a bloke in it, and she hops in with him. Of course, she's the unfaithful housewife, and the other guy's the lover. That's how they meet. There's so many of them doing it, you wonder they don't all bump into their mates out there. They could even form a club. "The Seven-Year Itch Society," and maybe rent a furnished flat together as a club room. It would certainly be a lot more comfortable than doing it in the backs of cars.

Jacqui didn't do any of the things she did out of wickedness. She used to feel sorry for the blokes she screwed with. When she came in from her curb crawlers, she would say that she was trying to help them. They were pathetic and unhappy, and she thought maybe by having sex with them she could cheer them up and make them feel loved and wanted.

She wasn't bad, she was just crazy.

Jacqui seemed to feel she had some sort of mission to all these guys. There's an idea you hear that prostitutes are a really important sort of psychiatrist. If it wasn't for them, all the little perverts would cause a lot of trouble. Instead of whipping prostitutes and having them dress up as little boys and girls, they'd attack real people and molest children.

Jacqui seemed to feel she should be like that. She might have been OK if she hadn't got hooked up with a bloke like me and got herself pregnant. She could have gone around all her life being picked up by these little bents and trying to cure their hangups by screwing with them.

She might even have got on really well, gone to the top. A lot of lords and ladies we have in this country now, the earls and things, their families started off with one of their female relatives doing it for everybody, and one day she dropped them for some king or other and was given a title and a big estate. Jacqui might have ended up like that, if she'd laid the top people.

Perhaps the whole business was *my* fault. I got too uptight and serious about everything. If I'd been more easygoing, I could maybe have turned a blind eye to what Jacqui was doing. Maybe I saw everything too black and white.

The truth is, we don't live in a *good* world like you get in the movies or the magazines. People aren't "good" or "bad," they're just all trying to keep themselves alive and make a decent life for their children. A married man with three little kids gets run over, but it isn't deliberate, it's just like the rest of life, an accident.

A man like me has a girl and a baby he loves, but ends up killing them both. It just happens.

Your whole life just happens to you, really. If you're lucky, then lucky things happen to you and you're happy. But if you're unlucky, there just isn't anything you can do about it, except maybe join the Spiritualists or the Buddhists, commit suicide, and hope you get a better deal next time around.

I sat and looked at Jacqui until dawn came up, thinking things like that and wondering what I ought to do with her. I had to do something. I couldn't leave her forever in the cold and the dark.

It reminded me of a time years ago, when I was in this little country churchyard with a girl called Brenda, and I found a little angel statue in a dark old shed.

Me and Brenda were looking for somewhere to be

private, if you know what I mean. We'd gone for a walk in the country together, and we both got this stupendous urge to have it away, right in the middle of this old village church we'd gone to look at. You know how it is, when you're out in the fresh air and it's a lovely sunny day, you get all loving toward one another and you can't wait.

The churchyard looked too public, and anyway the grass was wet, but we found this big old wooden hut hidden out among the trees and decided to go in there. And when I opened the door, there was this little angel standing there.

He was one of those churchyard angels they put over little kids' graves, and for some reason they'd taken him off the grave and put him in this dark shed. It seemed a really mean thing to do to him. He had a lovely little face, just like a pretty baby's, and he was holding a bunch of stone flowers in his little hand. Once upon a time he'd stood on a gravestone where he could see all around him and listen to the birds. And now he was left to molder in this old shed with the spiders and the earwigs.

I started to feel like that about Jacqui. I kept thinking of her lying at the bottom of the deep freeze, not able to see or hear anything. It was a very sad thing to be doing to anyone. I couldn't just leave her there forever, not when I felt sorry for the little statue. What I did, after me and Brenda were finished, was put him out in the graveyard, on a grave. He weighed about a ton, and I nearly ruptured myself lifting him, but I couldn't just leave him where he was.

No more than I could leave Jacqui where she was.

I wanted to do something nice for Jacqui. Certainly something much better than the authorities do for people.

The things they do to you when you're dead, in their mortuaries, are downright grotesque. We had a Scots bloke, once, driving for the firm, and he used to cut up bodies in Glasgow, before he moved down south.

The things he told us would make you go green. He was telling a bunch of us one of his yarns one day, and the girl on the telephone in the office passed right out on the floor. They have to examine all the vital organs of the body, so they take out the brain, the heart, the liver, and the rest. They get your brain out by taking the top of your head off, like a boiled egg. First they scalp you, then they drill two holes in your skull and put two screws in. That's so they can grip your head with a special tool, otherwise it's all bloody and it keeps slipping through their hands. Then they saw the top of your head off, to get at your brain.

To get your heart and stuff, they cut your stomach open, from your pubic area to your nipples, and drag all your guts out. The guts are no use, so they throw them in the incinerator. But your heart and your liver and your brain they put on a tray and send up to the laboratory for examination.

While your bits are being seen to, they sew the top of your head back on. There's no brain in it. That comes later. The tray full of bits comes back from the lab, and they dump the contents in your stomach and stitch it all up. If you've been in a morgue for any length of time, you're buried with your brain where your bowels should be.

Another thing, too, was the perverts you get in those places. You're always hearing stories of beautiful girls' bodies being violated in mortuaries. Every now and then one of them hits the papers, some mortuary attendant shagging the corpses. There's no knowing what some guys will do, they're so bent. Anyone who lets the authorities get their hands on his wife's body is asking for trouble.

Ordinary burial's not much better. It gives me the creeps, the thought of people being buried, it's such a tatty, morbid business. I taxi people down to funerals odd times, and I get to know the funeral men. It's all a big horselaugh to them, looking solemn while someone's being stuck in the ground. Just before the funeral they've had the cars at a wedding, and they're still sweeping confetti out of the motor at the churchyard. While the mourners are inside, the drivers are out in the porch doing the horses in *The Daily Mirror*. You check out any funeral man's jacket pockets, you'll find *The Daily Mirror*. They get the racing page and fold it up real small and put it in their pocket. Inside the church, some big nob's being given the burial service, and the old vicar's going on about what a marvelous sod he was, kind and loving and generous, and all that. (If he'd really been any of those things he could never have died with all the dough he had, but no one notices that.) And in the porch at the back, the funeral men have slipped out their *Mirrors* and they're muttering out the corner of their mouths, "How do you fancy 'Telephone Hill' in the three o'clock?" Either that, or they're eyeing up any good-looking birds in the party.

Then, when the body's in the ground, it's tips all around. They're all coughing and touching their fore-locks, everyone from the vicar to the gravedigger. The chief mourner takes them all to one side and drops them a fiver here, a couple of quid there, and the body's hardly even hit the bottom of the hole.

It was like that when they buried my mother. I didn't have sense enough then to stop them doing it.

It was dead dismal in the graveyard, really sick and miserable. There was a really nasty wind blowing, and it was trying to rain. They took the poor old girl in her box and dumped her in this hole in the ground, then everyone went off back to my house for a feed and a drink.

It was really squalid. They had the entire edge of the hole lined with flowers giving off this horrible sickly smell. I had a look down the hole when they'd all gone, and it was about as cheerful as an outside latrine. It had been pouring the night before, and the bottom of the grave was full of water. It was all sticky and dark and clayey and I could imagine all the slimy things there'd be in the ground, just waiting to eat my mother.

I've hated myself ever since for letting them do that to her. She spent twenty years bringing me up and caring for me, and that was her reward, that was all she got. I sure as hell wasn't going to do it to Jacqui. I was going to give her something much better than that.